He pushed on the lever, but the door wouldn't budge.

Cassie tried the other door. "This shouldn't be locked."

Shining the light through the slim window slat, he peered through it and saw metal chairs wedged beneath the handles—confirmation that this was a deliberate act.

At his hesitation, Cassie looked over his shoulder. The air seemed to leak out of her.

"I'm going to call the police." In the glare of her phone screen, he saw her frown. "I don't have service. Do you?"

He checked his phone, his gut hardening. "No. Whoever's behind this must be using a signal jammer."

"My attacker hasn't given up, has he?"

A scream echoed down the corridor, and Cassie grabbed his wrist. He wove his fingers through hers. "We stay together."

She nodded, her eyes huge in her face. They passed the deserted classrooms one after another. As they neared the library and principal's office, a flickering orange glow ate up the darkness.

"I smell smoke," Cassie whispered.

Luke's steps faltered. He tightened his grip on her hand, his mind and body rebelling.

"Luke, something's on fire..."

Karen Kirst was born and raised in East Tennessee near the Great Smoky Mountains. She's a lifelong lover of books, but it wasn't until after college that she had the grand idea to write one herself. Now she divides her time between being a wife, homeschooling mom and romance writer. Her favorite pastimes are reading, visiting tearooms and watching romantic comedies.

Books by Karen Kirst

Love Inspired Suspense

Explosive Reunion
Intensive Care Crisis
Danger in the Deep
Forgotten Secrets
Guarding His Child
Dangerous Ranch Threat

Smoky Mountain Defenders

Targeted for Revenge
Smoky Mountain Ambush
Mountain Murder Investigation
Witness Protection Breach

Visit the Author Profile page at LoveInspired.com for more titles.

DANGEROUS RANCH THREAT

KAREN KIRST

LOVE INSPIRED SUSPENSE
INSPIRATIONAL ROMANCE

LOVE INSPIRED® SUSPENSE
INSPIRATIONAL ROMANCE

Recycling programs for this product may not exist in your area.

ISBN-13: 978-1-335-59784-7

Dangerous Ranch Threat

For questions and comments about the quality of this book, please contact us at CustomerService@Harlequin.com.

Love Inspired
22 Adelaide St. West, 41st Floor
Toronto, Ontario M5H 4E3, Canada
www.LoveInspired.com

Printed in U.S.A.

To appoint unto them that mourn in Zion, to give unto them beauty for ashes, the oil of joy for mourning, the garment of praise for the spirit of heaviness; that they might be called trees of righteousness, the planting of the Lord, that he might be glorified.

—*Isaiah* 61:3

To my husband, Marek. I love you the most.

To my editor, Emily Rodmell.
Thank you for pulling me out of the slush pile and
guiding me all these years. I appreciate your hard work.

A big thank-you to Josh Felker for your input
in my FFA and agriculture teacher research.

ONE

Elated by the winter fundraiser's success, Cassie West hummed her way through the high school's barn. The clatter of a rake hitting the ground somewhere in the dark startled her into silence. Expecting another teacher or one of her students, she turned toward the door. The greeting died on her lips. A man hovered in the shadows, a ski mask covering all but his eyes. He lunged, snaked a belt around her throat and choked off her gasp.

Cassie clawed at his arms as he propelled her into a nearby stall. Her feet tangled in a coiled hose, and she sprawled on the straw-strewn dirt. Before she could summon help, her attacker pounced, silencing her again with the belt. His eyes gleamed. His brows pinched together in evil determination. Growing lightheaded, she fought to escape.

Why her? Why here? Why now?

She cried out to God. There was so much life left to live. Her parents needed her on the ranch. Her students and the agriculture program depended on her.

Lord, I thought I had more time.

"Cassie? You in here?"

Luke! Her ranch hand couldn't have come at a more welcome time.

She struck her boots against the floor, trying to make as

much noise as possible. An angry, guttural sound vibrated in her attacker's chest. Seconds later, he shoved off her and barreled through the opening. She heard Luke grunt and the barn door creak.

"Cassie!" Luke hurried into the stall and helped her sit up. "You all right?"

Her heart hammered in her chest. Gasping for breath, all she could manage was a brief nod.

"What happened?"

"I—I came in to clean up. I didn't hear anyone follow me inside. Maybe he was waiting for me?" A chill passed through her at the thought of him watching her. "He tried to strangle me."

Belatedly realizing she had a death grip on Luke's arm, she forced herself to release him.

"Come on, let's get you outside."

Luke helped her to her feet. She wobbled, and his arm came around her. "Steady now."

His voice was as gentle as the morning sunrise. She'd heard him talk in just that tone to her horses. In the aisle, the overhead light picked out the concern in his vivid blue eyes.

Luke Fisher was new to Tulip, and she was happy she'd hired him. He'd proven to be a kind, insightful, hardworking man. However, he shared very little about himself, which left her imagination to run wild. She had a lot of questions about the raven-haired cowboy.

Luke accompanied her to the side of the barn where the remnants of their fundraising efforts remained. The students and parents who'd stayed behind to clean up were packing the few pies that hadn't sold and stacking the folding tables onto the trailer.

Morgan Tucker, high school senior and president of their Future Farmers of America chapter, looked up at their approach. Her smile died when she caught sight of Cassie.

"What's wrong, Miss West?"

"Did anyone see a man leaving the barn just now?" Luke asked.

Morgan and the others shrugged and shook their heads. The main gathering had been in the grass beside the traditional barn. The older building and the newer open-air barn were connected by a covered walkway. From here, the people didn't have direct line of sight to the far doors, and her attacker could've easily snuck out the opposite way and escaped through the school's eight-acre farm.

"I'm going to have a look around," Luke told her. "Stay here."

He strode into the darkness as if hunting criminals was just another ranch chore. The few men who hadn't yet left spread out, prepared to defend the women and teens. Morgan and the others crowded around her, seeking reassurance.

She schooled her features and tried to bury her fear. "I'm fine," she told them.

Arianna Meadows, the high school guidance counselor, clearly didn't buy it. Her troubled gaze fell to Cassie's throat, which felt raw and probably bore the marks of her attack.

The crisp air deepened the chill in her bones. Cassie tugged her jacket collar up. "Let's finish cleaning. We have an early start again tomorrow."

While the students reluctantly returned to their tasks, Arianna hung back. "Someone attacked you?"

Cassie wished her legs would stop trembling. "If Luke hadn't come in when he did…"

Arianna put her arm around Cassie's shoulders. "You have to call the sheriff."

"I don't want to worry the students."

"We're almost finished here, anyway. I'll send them home after we return the tables to the cafeteria."

The bonfire had been left to putter out, and the outdoor heaters had been packed away. While Arianna hustled the students out of earshot, Cassie spoke with the dispatcher, who promised to send someone.

Luke returned grim-faced. "He's gone." His gaze traced the connected barns and outbuildings. "Why aren't there security cameras?"

"No room in the budget." Until tonight, she hadn't thought there was a need.

"The community obviously supports your program. Maybe they'd be willing to chip in."

He was right. The citizens of Tulip supported her students in multiple ways, not just financially. Many parents and school staff had stepped up to help coach their FFA teams. Although she was their teacher and chapter advisor, she didn't possess unlimited knowledge. She depended on others to fill in the gaps and give students a wide range of opportunities.

"Did anything stand out about your attacker?"

She thrust her fingers through her hair to smooth the tangles and remove bits of debris. "It happened too fast."

"What about his build? Any clues his clothing might tell you? Did you notice any specific smells?"

Luke fired off the questions in an authoritative manner that was unlike his usual style. Her surprise must've shown, because he visibly relaxed his shoulders.

"Just trying to help."

"It was dark in the stall, and with his mask..." She shrugged. "He was strong but not overly muscular. Taller than me."

"That's a good start. More details might come to you later."

She wanted to put the attack out of her mind, not dwell on it. "He had a belt."

His brows rose. "What color? Was the belt buckle unique?"

Her nails dug into her palms. "He wasn't wearing it. He used it to try to strangle me."

Fire kindled in Luke's eyes, and his jaw grew taut.

"I can't make sense of it," she continued. "Nothing like this has ever happened on school grounds."

"Can you think of anyone who might hold a grudge against you? Anyone who's angry enough to hurt you?"

"Hurt me? He wanted to *kill* me, Luke."

Unease balled in Luke's gut. He thought he'd left violence and crime behind in Texas. He was on an extended medical leave from the police department and had come to Tulip, Mississippi, on an unofficial mission to gather intel on the Wilder family. His interest in the Wilders was personal. No one in Tulip could know the real reason he was here until he'd decided if he was going to reveal his true identity or not.

The fear in Cassie's molten brown eyes made him want to punch something. During the five weeks he'd worked on her ranch, he'd learned that Cassidy West had a heart as big as his home state. She was devoted to her ranch and the animals it supported. She was also a high school teacher who poured everything she had into her students and their agriculture program. The fact he was using her to get to the Wilders bothered him. Now, when his conscience pricked him, it wasn't a needle. It was more like a knife blade.

The deputy's arrival curtailed Luke's questions. Probably a good thing, since Cassie had looked at him askance when his training had taken over. Deputy Hank Flowers was about five years past retirement, but he was thorough and treated Cassie like a favorite daughter.

Everyone seemed to like Cassie. It was no surprise that she couldn't come up with motives or suspects. Hank promised to have a look around in the morning in case there was something they'd missed.

"You okay to drive?" Luke asked.

Tucking a lock of her wavy blond hair behind her ear, she nodded. "I'm not going home, though. I've got to see Remi."

If she was heading to the Wilder ranch, he wanted to go along. This would be his first—and possibly only—opportunity to see the place. "I'll take you."

She bit her lower lip, and a crease formed between her honey-colored brows. "You're sure? You must be as exhausted as I am. It's been a long day."

"Positive." Ushering her to his truck, he gestured to her classic turquoise-and-white Ford pickup parked nearby. "I'll give you a ride back here to school in the morning."

"I appreciate it. To tell the truth, I'd rather not be alone just yet."

Seated behind the wheel, he pointed to the dash. "Adjust the heat to your liking."

She fastened her seat belt and scanned the surrounding fields. The football stadium sat between the farm and the high school. The greenhouse, also used for their agriculture program, was ahead on the left. Thick shadows gathered in the pastures between the greenhouse and barns.

She was wearing her official FFA blue corduroy jacket and pulled the sleeves down past her hands, curling her fingers inside. "Do you think he's out there hiding?"

"He's likely long gone by now."

Huddled in her jacket, her pretty face creased in fear, she pushed his instincts to serve and protect into overdrive. *Keep it professional, McCoy.* He had to avoid the hazard of personal engagement.

"You and Remi Wilder have been friends a long time, I gather?"

He already knew the answer, but she needed a distraction. Plus, she might reveal details he couldn't unearth on his own.

"Since kindergarten. Remi and I were in the same grade. Her brother, Nash, was three grades ahead of us, as was his fiancée, Skye Saddler. You met her at church, remember?"

Every interaction with the Wilder siblings had been carefully cataloged in his brain. "She's the one who traded her deputy uniform for a chef's apron. She has the food truck."

"Yep. Wait until you taste her waffles. She only operates the food truck for special occasions during the winter. If you're here come spring, you'll have to pay her a visit."

He heard her unspoken question. Cassie had respected his privacy up until now, even though her curiosity was unmistakable.

"I never know where the wind will take me." At her frown, he tacked on, "But I'll be sure to take your advice if I'm still here."

The job on her ranch had all but fallen into his lap. Before coming to Tulip, he'd done a deep dive into Nash and Remi Wilder, which included information about the people closest to them. He'd been hanging out at the Pit Stop Café for the third day in a row when he'd overheard a conversation between Cassie and some wizened cowboys. Her parents had had to rush off to Florida to care for an elderly relative, leaving Cassie in a bind. Luke had seen an opportunity to get close to the Wilders' inner circle. Silently thanking his uncle for all those summers working on his farm, he'd offered his services.

The dawn to dusk ranch chores had proven useful in another way, too. Since he'd started working for Cassie, he'd been too busy and exhausted to dwell on his partner's death or the fact he was to blame.

"Did he hurt you when he barreled by you?"

Cassie's voice scattered his thoughts, and he realized

he'd been rubbing his aching shoulder. He was certain his surgeon wouldn't approve of the manual labor he'd been doing these past weeks. "He knocked into me. It was nothing."

The entrance gate to the Wilder ranch loomed in his headlights. As he drove past the ranch store, paddocks and multiple structures, he wondered what it might've been like to grow up here.

"Remi's fixing up her grandparents' old place," Cassie told him. "You'll have to take the dirt road beside the ranch house—" Breaking off, she leaned forward. "Wait, that's her truck. She must be visiting Nash."

Luke parked behind the other vehicles, adrenaline washing through his system. He hadn't done much undercover work during his time as detective, but he'd learned to keep his personal thoughts about a case or criminal tucked away beneath a professional veneer. He prayed that ability would serve him well in this instance.

He trailed behind Cassie, picking up details about the white and black ranch house. Nash answered the door and ushered them through the foyer, past the formal dining room and into the shared living and kitchen area. Remi rounded the bar brandishing a spatula. Her smile was welcoming. The siblings had similar coloring, both with blond hair and electric-blue eyes.

"Did we catch you at a bad time?" Cassie locked her fingers together at her waist.

"Eden is fast asleep," Remi said, speaking of Nash's young daughter. "The fundraiser wore her out. I was about to serve pie. Did you see that Nash bought four?"

"I had to get one of each," he said, grinning. "It's for a good cause."

"Yeah, your sweet tooth," Remi retorted. "Would either of you like a piece?"

"None for me, thanks." Luke sidled closer to Cassie, whose complexion was too pale for his liking. "Unfortunately, we're not here for a social visit. There was an incident after you left."

Remi's smile slipped. "What happened?"

Cassie cleared her throat. "I was attacked."

Tossing the spatula in the sink, Remi crossed the room and clasped Cassie's hands. "Tell me everything."

Nash came close, too, his rugged features wreathed in concern as Cassie relayed the details.

"He got away," Luke told them. "We don't have witnesses or security footage."

Remi studied him. Was her cop radar sounding an alarm? Would she figure out he wasn't the roaming, rootless cowboy everyone assumed he was? She'd worked undercover for the Atlanta PD's narcotic unit before moving back home and hiring onto nearby Mayfield's department.

"Luke intervened," Cassie said, her gratitude evident. "He even searched for the guy."

"There are many avenues of escape on that farm," Nash pointed out. "The pastures back up to privately owned land that's not currently in use. He could've left his vehicle any number of places and gone undetected."

"Has there been a pattern of similar crimes in Tulip?" Luke asked.

Remi and Nash exchanged a look. He already knew about the trouble Nash encountered last spring. Several news outlets had reported about the attempts on his and Skye Saddler's lives. Thankfully, the culprit had been caught and sent to prison.

"Tulip is for the most part a peaceful place." Nash put his hand on Cassie's shoulder. "Do you want to stay the night? You and Remi can share the guest bedroom."

"Like old times." There was no mistaking Remi's affection for her best friend.

"As much as I'd love an impromptu slumber party, I have school tomorrow."

"I'll keep an eye on her," Luke promised.

The siblings stared at him. They clearly thought of Cassie as family and were determined to protect her. He could practically see them sizing him up, trying to decide if he was worthy of their trust.

He shifted uncomfortably. Could they see anything in him that might tip them off? He took after his mom's side of the family in all ways but one—the distinctive Wilder blue eyes. But there was always the possibility he might resemble an uncle, grandfather or cousin.

Luke wasn't ready to reveal his secret. He had a lot of information yet to gather. Only when he was certain of the outcome would he decide whether to try and build a relationship with his half siblings or walk away.

After more than a month in Tulip, he was starting to feel it might not be as easy to leave as he'd originally thought.

TWO

Remi pulled Cassie into the kitchen and leaned in close. "I'm not sure we should trust Luke to keep you safe."

"I wouldn't be here if not for him."

She cocked her head, her high blond ponytail swishing impatiently. "What do we really know about him, though?"

The men had wandered over to the fireplace, and Nash was explaining the various photos and magazine clippings pertaining to the Wilder legacy. Cassie focused in on Luke, who was again massaging his shoulder without seeming to be aware of it. He was like every other cowboy she'd ever known—courteous, hardworking and tough. Sun-bronzed from his outdoor work, he dressed in flannel shirts, worn-in jeans and cowboy boots. Unlike the men in town, this raven-haired, blue-eyed cowboy stirred her imagination. His smile made her heart race. His presence on her ranch made her think about leaping into the dating pool—with him.

Cassie didn't intend to act on the foolish impulse. Luke wasn't the sticking-around kind, and he didn't seem to be interested in a short-term romance. Neither was she. She wasn't sure she was ready for romance at all.

"I may not know a lot, but I know he's a good man," she said. "He's been an answer to my prayers."

"I thought you were hasty in hiring a stranger, and I

haven't changed my mind about that." Remi crossed her arms and leaned against the sink. "There's something about him that bothers me. I just can't put my finger on it."

"You're thinking like a cop."

"Yeah. So?"

"At some point, you have to stop viewing the new people you come across as potential cases to solve."

"And you have to stop taking everyone at their word."

Cassie grimaced. She'd been guilty of being naïve in the past. After all, she'd believed Brian had meant it when he'd said he wanted to marry her.

Remi frowned. "I didn't mean to bring up bad memories. I admire your optimism, truly. I simply don't want you to get hurt. Did you check his references?"

Cassie's cheeks burned.

Remi's brows shot up. "You didn't get any?"

"I was desperate." She spread her hands wide. "The ranch can't run itself."

Her work as an agriculture teacher wasn't confined to school hours. Because of their FFA program, she spent many evenings and weekends assisting students. That usually left the bulk of the ranch chores to her parents. When her grandmother broke her hip, Cassie's parents had hopped on the first plane. Her recovery was going slower than planned, and they were considering selling her house and moving her into an assisted living complex. The logistics of that made Cassie's head spin.

"I'll do a background check on him."

"Remi, no." Cassie shot a glance at the men. "He's a very private person. I don't want to repay his hard work by delving into affairs that don't concern me."

Remi opened her mouth to argue, and Cassie held up her hand. "I'm going home. I have a full day tomorrow, and three of my students are taking part in a speech competition in Mayfield tomorrow night."

"I'll be checking in on you."

"That's nothing new."

The siblings hugged Cassie goodbye and cautiously accepted Luke's vow to watch over her and the ranch. They were being more overprotective than usual, but who could blame them? Her parents were out of town, and she'd been attacked. She knew Nash was extra sensitive when those he cared about were in danger, thanks to his recent experience with Skye and little Eden.

Cassie trusted Luke, and they would, too, in time.

Luke was quiet on the drive home. The silence was comfortable between them, and soft Christian music on the radio soothed her frayed nerves.

Her family ranch was on the opposite side of town and about a tenth the size of the Wilders' enterprise. Her father was in it for the love of the land and lifestyle and nothing more. They had a hundred head of beef cattle, four horses, a passel of pigs and chickens, an unspecified number of barn cats and one very special dog. Cassie loved the place as much as her parents did. After her engagement fell through, she'd chosen to move out of her parents' place, purchase a tiny home and park it on the ranch instead of moving elsewhere in Tulip.

The barn and surrounding outbuildings were clearly outlined by the utility pole light. Her parents' brick ranch house and her own little place beneath the trees off to the right were wreathed in shadows. Instead of parking near the barn where he bunked in the loft apartment, he pulled up to her front door.

A ring of shoulder-high hedges formed the border of her private, outdoor garden oasis where she enjoyed her morning coffee and spent evenings unwinding with a book during warmer months. Because of the attack, she now saw it as a potential place for someone to hide.

Luke turned off the engine and held out his hand. "Give me your keys."

If she were Remi or Skye, she'd turn down his help and inspect her home herself. But she wasn't a cop, and she'd lived in a naïve bubble of innocence her entire life.

Grateful for his presence, she placed the keys in his palm, her knuckles skimming his warm, calloused skin. Goose bumps shimmered up her arm at the unexpected contact. Averting her face, she threaded her fingers through her hair and scolded herself for the reaction.

Cassie remained in the truck while Luke entered her home. The inspection didn't take long, of course, since the space was composed of a compact living room and kitchen combo, bathroom and single bedroom on the main floor and twin lofts for storage on either side. The outside light in her garden flickered on, shining around the pointy hedge tips. Minutes later, he appeared in the doorway and waved her over.

The crisp air wrapped around her as she darted from the truck to the door. Her goldendoodle, Dusty, trotted over from the barn, long, fluffy tail wagging in greeting.

Luke set the keys on her butcher block counter. "You're all set. I'm going to look around the property before retiring for the night. Call if you need me."

This was his first time inside her home, and his size and energy seemed to shrink the space. His scent reminded her of rain-washed mornings in her favorite spot on the ranch, a meadow by the stream that smelled woodsy and fresh and faintly of pine. Was he the type to buy cologne or just good-smelling shaving cream? There was so much she didn't know about him, and so much she wanted to learn.

"Thanks, Luke."

He inclined his head. "Good night."

Cassie locked the door behind him and went to check the other exit. It was located in her bedroom and led out to her garden space. What had he thought of her minimalistic style? White was the predominate color throughout the space, punctuated with natural woods and pops of her favorite color: green. He must not mind living simply, either, because the barn loft apartment was outfitted only with essentials. As she got ready for bed, she wondered about his past, where he'd grown up and why he lived like a nomad.

She settled into bed with her Bible and read some of her favorite Psalms, her gaze drawn to the many verses she'd underlined. She fell asleep praying and wasn't sure how much time had passed when Dusty's growls jerked her awake.

Cassie lay there for a time trying to soothe Dusty with soft reassurances. Then came a rattle of the front doorknob. She bolted upright. Barking ferociously, Dusty raced into the living room. Cassie scrambled out of the bed, crept past the bathroom and slid a knife from the kitchen drawer. The knob rattled again, and she heard what sounded like a shoulder thumping against the wood.

Dusty jumped, his front paws slamming against the door. The rattling stopped.

Cassie went in search of her phone. As she entered the bedroom, that door's knob rattled. The knife slipped from her fingers and clattered to the floor, barely missing her foot. Her dog raced past her, his barks bouncing off the walls. She unlocked her phone screen with shaking fingers and managed to locate Luke's contact info.

He answered on the second ring, his voice muffled.

"Someone's here," she whispered.

He probably couldn't hear her, but he surely heard the racket her dog was making.

"Be right there."

There was a sliding noise, then a click. The knob turned, and the door began to open.

Cassie crouched on the floor and located the knife, prepared to fend off whoever came through the door.

Luke threw on his clothes and boots and grabbed his pistol from the nightstand drawer. He could hear Dusty barking as soon as he emerged from the barn. Racing past the main house, he prayed for God's intervention. There was no telling what he might find inside Cassie's home. His mind went into trauma mode, conjuring up tragic images that made his heart squeeze with dread.

Please, Lord, don't let me fail her like I failed Simon.

The front door was locked. He circled the entire structure, anticipating a violent encounter. He sidled between the hedges and the wall and entered the garden. It was empty. This door was locked, too.

"Cassie? It's me, Luke."

When she didn't immediately respond, he pounded on the door and called her name. He was about to kick it in when she opened it a crack. Her eyes were huge, her blond hair a disheveled cloud around her face.

Dusty wormed through the opening and would've raced into the night if Luke hadn't caught his collar. He wrangled the furry canine inside and locked the door behind him.

Dusty fell silent, and Luke could hear Cassie's rapid breathing. He tucked his gun in his rear waistband and held out his hand. "I'll take that."

She looked down and stared at the knife in her grip.

Luke took it from her cold fingers, set it on the nightstand and gently grasped her shoulders. "You're safe, Cassie. Whoever was out there is gone."

"He got the door open." Her lips trembled. "I don't know

how. I've seen things on television. Maybe he used a credit card."

"Did he make it inside?"

"Dusty rushed into the opening and snapped at him before he could. I don't know if he bit him."

"I'm going to look around."

She gripped his sides, her fingers twisting his T-shirt. "Don't go."

Acting on instinct, he pulled her close, tucked her head against his chest and wrapped his arms around her.

"You're going to be okay," he said quietly.

But he couldn't guarantee it, could he?

She stayed in his arms for a while, and he rested his chin atop her head. She smelled nice, like the roses in his mom's garden. She fit against him as if she were made to be there, soft and snuggly. Cassie was easy to be around, which was unexpected considering they were practically strangers.

When she shifted out of his arms, he felt a pang of regret. He belatedly noticed how inviting she looked in her long-sleeved pink shirt and matching pink pants with cute dogs on them. Her feet were bare, and her toenails were painted bright pink.

"I don't know how I'm going to sleep now," she said, avoiding his gaze.

"Why don't you stay at your parents' tonight?"

Her brow creased. "I don't know."

"I'll sleep in the guest bedroom if you want."

"You'd do that?"

"Of course. As your employee, I'm committed not only to the safety of your property and animals, but yours as well."

He needed to remind himself that their relationship was of a professional nature. He couldn't start thinking of her as a friend.

Lord, I didn't realize when I started this mission that my actions might hurt someone.

They made the short trek to the main house without incident. Cassie gave him a quick tour. Unlike her place, her parents' house had a more traditional style with shiny hardwood floors, neutral walls and dark fabric couches with nailhead trim and sturdy wooden frames. Heaps of floral pillows invited guests to relax. Stacks of home decorating magazines dominated the coffee table, and framed photographs on the fireplace mantel told the story of Cassie's childhood. A pair of bedrooms and a bathroom were on their right, and the primary bedroom and en suite were on the left. The living room flowed into a kitchen with honey-hued wood cabinets and granite counters. A sunroom had been tacked onto the back, reachable through the dining nook.

As soon as they checked all the doors and windows, Cassie directed him to the guest bedroom and told him good night. He didn't sleep well, and he doubted she did, either.

The next morning, after they conquered the chores together, they shared a pot of coffee and cinnamon muffins. Her sunflower-yellow shirt, paired with jeans and brown leather lace-up work boots, complemented her skin tone and dark eyes. She wore her blue corduroy FFA jacket over it, and her hair spilled over her shoulders in a river of gold. She was a beautiful woman, he let himself acknowledge. Although they'd been in each other's company plenty of times, he'd been laser focused on his goals and hadn't given in to curiosity about Remi Wilder's best friend.

He rinsed out his coffee cup and placed it on the dish rack. "You have to leave at half past six, right?"

She threw her napkin in the trash can. "Not today. I texted Thomas Keller and asked him to go to school early and feed the animals for me."

That gave him pause. Cassie wasn't the type to delegate her duties. It revealed just how bothered she was by the attacks. "He's a student?"

"Former student. Thomas graduated two years ago and is attending community college. He volunteers at the barn."

"You and he get along?"

Her brow creased. "Yes, of course. Like Morgan, he was one of those students who wasn't sure if he was interested in the agriculture side of things. I encouraged them both during their freshman years, and they turned into natural leaders. He served in several different positions in our FFA chapter, including vice president and president."

"So you can't see him as being the one who attacked you?"

"Never." Her eyes widened. "Thomas is an upstanding young man."

Luke kept his cynical thoughts to himself. He'd learned people weren't always what they seemed to be. He certainly wasn't who he'd led Cassie to believe he was.

When they arrived at the school, he decided to accompany her inside. This wasn't his case, but he could do some reconnaissance, just in case Deputy Flowers didn't do his due diligence.

"You're walking me to class?"

"I've never seen where you work."

"Brace yourself."

He didn't know what she was referring to until they entered the building and were engulfed in a sea of teenagers. The guys mostly ignored them. The girls gathered around them, seeking an introduction. Luke's neck began to burn. Their blushes and giggles brought a knowing smirk to Cassie's face.

"Time to get to class, ladies."

After the girls reluctantly scattered, Luke said, "I take it you don't get many visitors."

"Not ones who look like Hollywood stars," she quipped.

He arched a brow, and she blushed to the roots of her hair.

"The building is shaped like a U. Along this entry hall, we have the nurse's office, bathrooms, custodial closet and cafeteria." She pointed to the double doors at the left end. "That's the auditorium, and down that far wing are the math, English and history classrooms. The gym is down there, as well as the music room." As they passed the cafeteria, he could see through the light-filled eating space to the windows overlooking a central courtyard. There were tables situated beneath several mature trees. "The main office is here, along with the principal's." She gestured to the right corner.

Walking along the other wing, she pointed out the library and foreign language and art rooms. "The science labs are across from my classroom."

Luke homed in on a man stationed in the doorway of Cassie's room. Possibly in his late thirties or early forties, he had buzzed blond hair, smoky-gray eyes and a goatee. He watched their approach with a furrowed brow.

"Good morning, Fallon."

"Cassie." He moved aside to let them pass and then followed them inside. "What happened last night? Titus came home and said you were upset. He said he saw the deputy arrive on school grounds."

"Fallon, I don't believe you've met my ranch hand, Luke Fisher." She turned to Luke. "Fallon teaches science. His son, Titus, is an ag student and was there last night." She set her book bag on her desk, removed her jacket and draped it on the back of her chair. "I was hoping to shield the students from the fact I was attacked last night."

Shock rippled across Fallon's face. "Did you catch the person responsible?"

"Unfortunately, no. I'd appreciate it if you'd keep this under your hat."

"Are the students in danger?"

Her features creased. "Considering he came after me a second time late last night, it's safe to say I'm the target."

A brunette in a blue dress suit breezed in, her heels clicking against the shiny tile. Luke had seen her at the fundraiser and had heard someone say she was the high school principal.

Her dark gaze swept over them with a hint of impatience. "Fallon, there are students unsupervised in your classroom."

Frowning, Fallon glanced at his smart watch and strode from the room.

"I'm hearing tidbits of troubling gossip about the fundraiser. I didn't notice anything out of the ordinary while I was there."

Cassie hurriedly introduced her to Luke as Gabriela Martinez. After relaying the details of the events, she added, "I should've contacted you last night."

"I'm just glad you're all right. Do the police have any leads?"

"Hank is supposed to have a look around this morning."

Gabriela planted her hands on her hips. "The other teachers have to be informed."

"The news will spread quickly."

"That might not be a bad thing," Luke interjected. "People will know to be on the lookout for anyone suspicious."

Gabriela nodded her agreement. "We'll have a teachers' meeting right after school today."

A pair of lanky boys sauntered in and slung their backpacks on desks in the back row. Gabriela gave Luke a pointed stare. "It's almost time for school to start."

"Mrs. Martinez?" A young redhead poked her head inside. "The secretary said your first appointment is here."

"Coming." Gabriela stalked from the room, high heels clicking furiously.

Luke tapped his Stetson against his thigh. "I have to get back to the ranch. I'll see you after school."

"I'm not coming straight home. I'm taking several students to Mayfield for a speech competition."

Normally, this wouldn't be a problem. Her schedule was her own business. However, after two attacks in one day, Luke was worried.

"I was planning to make a run to the supply store this afternoon, but I can go this morning and have everything unloaded in time to accompany you."

"That's really kind of you, Luke. I don't want to disrupt your schedule. I'll be with the students the whole time, anyway."

"I don't mind." And he didn't.

"You won't be bored?"

Boring wasn't a word he associated with Cassidy West. "I'm easily entertained."

"If you say so. Thanks, Luke."

Outside in the parking lot, he intercepted Deputy Hank Flowers. "Morning, Deputy. I don't know if you remember me—"

"Oh, I have a mind like a steel trap. Luke Fisher, right?"

"That's right."

"What can I do for you?"

He told him about the close call on the ranch. "I was wondering if you found any evidence here?"

The deputy tugged his waistband farther up his paunch. "I hate to think of sweet Cassie having to deal with this. As I feared, I didn't find a single helpful thing."

"Not a footprint or piece of clothing snagged on a nail? Tire tracks?"

"The problem is there were dozens of people here last

night. There's no way to distinguish one set of tracks or shoe prints from another."

Luke thought that was an excuse for laziness and decided to have a look around for himself. He accepted that his reason for being in Tulip would have to take a temporary back seat. Cassie's safety had to take priority because he was an officer of the law, not because he had feelings for his new boss.

THREE

Cassie had tasked Thomas with her morning chores. That wasn't an option for her third period class. The students chatted happily as they streamed into the open-air barn and spread out among the stalls, greeting the goats, sheep and pigs in their care. She lagged behind, her attention on the weathered barn. She couldn't avoid it forever. Best to get it over with. Gritting her teeth, she forced herself to enter.

The earthy smells of aged timber, leather and straw were familiar, but they had lost their ability to impart comfort. This building represented everything she loved about her life—connection to the land and the animals she'd been raised to value and the opportunity to share those values with her students. One brief yet violent encounter threatened to erase those good memories.

God, I need Your help. I'm scared, but I'm also angry. I don't know why this is happening or who's behind it, but I know You love me and care for me. Please give me courage.

Fisting her hands, she walked farther into the space and stared into the stall where her innocent, naïve view of the world had been shattered. Her stomach balled into a hard rock. Her breathing accelerated. At the sound of someone coming in the opposite door, she jumped and made a squeaking sound like a frightened mouse.

Thomas, her former student, stopped short. "Miss West. I'm sorry I startled you."

Pressing her hand to her chest, she said, "It's okay, Thomas." She took a deep breath. "Thanks for coming in this morning."

"I didn't mind." He put the rake he carried into the tack room.

"I thought you had class at this time."

Closing the tack room door, he lifted his ball cap and ran his fingers through his wavy brown hair. "You've never asked me to fill in for you before, and I thought maybe you were sick and might need me today."

"I wish you hadn't skipped on my account."

"We have a sub today anyway. He'll email our homework assignments to us." His clear green eyes studied her. "I heard what happened. Are you all right?"

She jutted her chin. "I will be."

Titus appeared in the other doorway, holding on to the frame and leaning inside. "We're out of rabbit pellets."

"Did you look in the feed room?"

"Yes, ma'am. And the room where we keep the smaller animals."

She removed a key from her key ring and handed it to him. "Go and look inside the storage shed. Ask Morgan to consult our supply list and whether a trip to the co-op is necessary."

"On it."

"I'm going out to the horse barn," Thomas said. "Unless you need me to do something else?"

"Have I told you lately how much I appreciate your help?"

He blushed and focused on his boots. "It's my pleasure."

Cassie joined the teenagers, who were feeding, washing and cuddling their animals. While her anxiety didn't entirely disappear, she was able to get through the rest of the day without falling apart. As expected, the teacher's meeting was uncomfortable. She didn't like being the center of attention, especially for something that left her feeling vulnerable and uncertain.

After the meeting ended, she saw that she had a missed call from Luke. He was supposed to be in the parking lot waiting for her. She went into the hallway and returned his call.

"I'm not going to make it," Luke said in way of a greeting. "One of the pregnant heifers is sick. I'm going to have to stay and keep an eye on her. I'm sorry, Cassie."

His voice was heavy with regret.

"I understand."

"Text me when you get there and again when you leave."

His obvious concern warmed her like a fire on a frosty night. Then she remembered what he'd said the night before. She was his employer, and in his mind, she fell under the umbrella of required duties. He didn't have a crush on her. Didn't want to know her beyond what was essential to do his job.

As Cassie drove the three teens to Mayfield, she mulled over her reaction to Luke Fisher. Living in a small town meant she'd grown up with just about all the eligible bachelors. There was nothing new or exciting about them, and they thought the same about her, she was certain. The reason she was preoccupied with Luke had to be because he was an unknown. He was mysterious when everything about her life in Tulip was routine.

They entered the outer ring of the business district and quickly located the office building where the speech competition was being held. Thirty-six students were set to take part. The top two competitors would move on to the state competitions. Cassie got wrapped up in the excitement of the program. Morgan, Titus and Jane were three of her most active, faithful students in the FFA program, and she was bursting with pride. When Titus seized the second place slot, she clapped and cheered as if he were her own son. Morgan and Jane accepted their loss with grace. Both girls had won competitions on their other teams and expressed sincere happiness for Titus's win.

While Jane caught up with an old friend and Titus spoke with the judges, Cassie and Morgan headed outside to start the truck and get the heater going.

"I'm starving," Morgan said, twisting her long brown hair into a bun and poking a pencil through it. "Can we stop at Marco's Pizza Palace?"

"That sounds fun," Cassie agreed, her good mood deflating a little when she found the parking lot already deserted. There were only a handful of vehicles left. The surrounding buildings appeared to be closed for the night. As they neared her truck, she noticed all four tires were flat.

Apprehension arrowed through her. "Morgan, go inside."

Her gray eyes clouded. "What's wrong?"

"Go inside and get Mr. O'Brien. Tell him I need him. Hurry."

"O-okay."

Cassie fished her phone from her pocket, intending to contact the police. Once Morgan was safely inside, she bent to inspect the tires. Sure enough, the slashes indicated this was no accident.

She unlocked her phone screen and was about to dial 911 when a hand clamped over her mouth. Her scream was muffled as the man fastened his arm around her middle, boosted her so that her feet didn't touch the ground and began to haul her around the side of the building. The alley between the buildings was dark and desolate and loomed like an awaiting nightmare.

Cassie kicked and writhed. He grunted as he tried to maintain his grip. He removed his hand from her mouth, wrapped both arms around her and towed her farther into the shadows. She screamed and thrashed her arms, occasionally landing a blow to his muscular body. But he kept on going. Deeper and deeper into the cavern. Farther and farther away from people and possible rescue.

The stench of rotting garbage invaded her nostrils. Between that and the pressure on her stomach, she gagged.

He was almost to the corner. Did he have a getaway vehicle waiting out of sight? Or did he plan to strangle her into eternal silence once they were far enough from the others?

Horror clawed at her as those seconds of sheer agony in the barn replayed in her mind.

"Hey! Stop!"

At the sound of Morgan's voice, Cassie's fear magnified by a thousand. She had to protect her student.

Cassie fought with renewed determination. Her captor wasn't tiring, however.

She was outmatched, and she wasn't sure if escape was an option.

Police officials and bystanders craned their necks to stare as Luke whipped into the parking lot. He wasn't familiar with Mayfield, and he was sure the navigation system had taken him the long way around. The strain in Cassie's voice when she'd asked him to come scraped at his conscience. He should've been here. He'd let her down, just like he had Simon.

He wound through the crowd, only to be blocked by an officer. "This is an active scene, sir. You'll have to wait over there."

Luke's first instinct was to whip out his police badge. He couldn't very well announce his profession, though. Morgan Tucker was nearby being comforted by her father, Evan, as well as two students he recognized from the fundraiser.

"Cassidy West is my boss. She asked me to come."

The officer consulted with someone over his radio and pointed out the lone ambulance parked beside the alley. Luke jogged over, his heart in his throat, flashes of his own hazy, pain-jarring ride to the hospital not that long ago. The burned patches across his torso seemed to pinch, reminding him of being locked in a burning garage with his partner and their desperate search for escape.

When he saw Cassie sitting inside the ambulance rather than strapped to a gurney, the tightness in his throat eased a little.

"Cassie."

Her head whipped up, and her brown eyes glittered with unshed tears. Luke sat down, put his arm around her and hugged her against him. Her body trembled. Her tears made him feel helpless, and he was overcome with the need to protect her. He thought of his younger sister, Paige, and how furious he'd be if she were in this situation. Of course, he didn't view Cassie like a sister. Not in the least.

She pulled away, averted her face and swiped at her cheeks.

"Do you need to go to the hospital?"

"No."

"Did the police already interview you?"

She nodded. "I wasn't much help. H-He grabbed me from behind. Mr. O'Brien said he was wearing a ski mask."

"Mr. O'Brien?"

Hooking her hair behind her ear, she met his gaze. "He's the lead organizer. When I saw my slashed tires, I sent Morgan inside to get him. Their appearance in the alley scared off my attacker."

Her eyes were bloodshot, and her nose was pink. When he'd left her that morning at school, her blond hair was a neat, gleaming curtain and her pink lipstick fresh. Now, the strands were straggly, and the lip color had been wiped away. She still managed to steal his breath.

"Morgan witnessed everything," she said heavily, fresh tears threatening. "I feel awful about it. How's this going to affect her?"

"She has her parents. Her father's here with her. She has her friends, and she has you." He'd seen the respect and genuine fondness the students had for Cassie.

"Her mom's not in the picture. She took off a few years ago and never looked back. But Evan's been dating Arianna for almost a year, and things are going great. Morgan and Arianna get along really well."

Cassie had introduced him to the guidance counselor, and he'd seen the redhead with Evan at church and the Pit Stop.

"You see? She has a solid support system, as do you." He paused, considering his next words. "Don't you think it's time to tell your folks what's going on?"

If her parents did decide to return, he would no longer have a valid reason to stay in Tulip.

"They've got their hands full with my grandmother."

"It will be better coming from you rather than one of their friends or neighbors. This will make the rounds on news outlets. Teenagers talk. It will be across Tulip soon."

"I guess you're right. I'll call them in the morning." She slowly stood. "I'm ready to go home."

"Not to Remi's?"

"I don't want to bother her again."

"I doubt she'd see it as a bother."

"I'll call her tomorrow, too." Brow creasing, she looked at her watch. "I forgot about my truck. I'll have to purchase tires."

"The police will have to process it for evidence anyway.

I'll give you a ride home, and we can return sometime tomorrow."

The paramedic appeared with a clipboard. After Cassie signed some papers, she told her she was free to go. As they were preparing to leave, a balding older man in a wrinkled brown suit handed Cassie his business card.

"Contact me if you remember anything else, Miss West." The man slipped his hand in his pants pocket, allowing his jacket to gape open and reveal his service weapon. There were stains on his tie, which was askew.

"Detective Kane, this is my employee, Luke Fisher. He was there during the other incidents."

The detective pulled out his notebook. "Is this a convenient time to answer some questions, Mr. Fisher?"

"Sure."

Luke's answers didn't impress Detective Kane, who rubbed the back of his neck and shook his head. "Not much to go on, I'm afraid."

"Are there any security or traffic cams in this area?" Luke asked.

"There aren't on either of these buildings. This isn't a high traffic area. I doubt we'll have any footage."

"But you'll check?"

His gaze sparked. "Yes, of course."

"I noticed a convenience store two blocks away on my drive in," Luke added. "He could've stopped there. Are there any gas stations nearby?"

"My team and I will research it. You can count on us to do a thorough job, Mr. Fisher."

"You'll be in touch with your findings?"

He jutted his chin. "Yes, Mr. Fisher."

Luke itched to be part of the investigation. Even if he did reveal his true identity, there was no guarantee the department would agree to allow his participation. It was up to the chief's discretion, as well as Detective Kane's.

"You watch a lot of crime shows or something?" Cassie asked when the detective left.

"Something like that."

Luke was starting to regret concealing the truth from Cassie. She was as honest as they came, and he knew she'd be hurt if she found out.

Luke hadn't made a decision yet about Nash and Remi. If he decided against telling them he was their long-lost sibling, he would have to leave Tulip for good and let everyone continue to believe he was a roaming cowboy, blowing into town for a few weeks and continuing on his journey.

One thing was certain—he couldn't leave until he knew Cassie was safe.

FOUR

Cassie put down the curry comb and reached for the dandy brush. Buck probably wondered why he was getting groomed so late and why she wasn't showering him with hugs and kisses. She'd led him out of his stall and crosstied him in the aisle. Dusty sat in the corner, his brown eyes fixed on her as if waiting for her to crumple to the ground. Her legs felt weak, and her hands were unsteady. After two attacks and one attempted home intrusion, she wasn't sure if she'd ever feel normal again.

Hearing Luke's footsteps on the stairs, she lowered the brush and watched him descend. He'd shed his brown, fleece-lined jacket and flannel shirt. The ivory Henley showed off his molded physique and complemented his golden skin and jet-black hair.

His astute gaze evaluated her as he held out a steaming stoneware mug. "I fixed you hot tea. Do you like peppermint?"

"I do. Thank you." Setting the brush on the shelf, she accepted the mug and sipped the bracing, slightly sweet brew. "I didn't figure you for a tea guy."

"My mom keeps the cabinets stocked in fall and winter. My sister and I had some every night."

This was one of the few personal details he'd shared. She

seized the opportunity to pry since it was also a chance to avoid talking about the latest attack.

"Do you have just the one sibling?"

Luke hesitated, his gaze shifting to her horse. He trailed his fingers down Buck's nose. "Paige is a character. I'm not sure I could handle any more."

"Is she older? Younger?"

"Younger. She's a senior in college."

"Are you close to her and your parents?"

He nodded. "I was blessed with a happy childhood. My mom and stepdad are wonderful people."

"Was your biological father in the picture?"

His expression shuttered. "I never met him."

Cassie curbed further questions, sensing the topic was a touchy one. She was surprised when he continued.

"My mom married my stepdad when I was two. He's the only father I've ever known."

"I'm close to my parents, too. I would've liked siblings, but it wasn't meant to be."

"Remi's like a sister to you, though."

"That's true. She was young when her and Nash's mother died, and she sort of adopted my mother. She spent more time here than at her own home."

"Her father didn't object to that?" There was an odd note in Luke's voice.

"Wes Wilder was a complicated man. He wasn't very involved with Remi. On the flip side, he was much too hard on Nash. I'm not sure which was worse. They each wrestle with different issues because of his actions."

He dropped his hand and stepped away from Buck. "He never remarried?"

"No. I don't remember him dating after Glory's death. Surprising, considering his standing in the community. He would've been considered a catch for the single women interested in financial security."

"How did Nash and Remi take his passing?"

"His death was unexpected. He died of a heart attack right there on the ranch. Nash was in the military at the time. Wes's death brought him back to Tulip for good. He's made his peace with it. Remi wrestles with conflicting emotions. She doesn't mourn him like she did her mom, and that makes her feel guilty."

She took another long sip of tea, wondering how he'd steered the conversation off himself without her noticing. "How did you end up in Tulip?"

"My family and I used to vacation in Gulfport. I've always wanted to explore more of the state. The road signs led me here." He flashed a sudden, disarming grin.

Her stomach flipped over. "Doesn't your family miss you?"

"My family is very important to me. I make time to see them."

"What about friends or girlfriends? Don't tell me you've left a string of broken hearts in your wake."

"That's not my style."

During his brief time in town, he'd caught the eye of plenty of women, but he hadn't seemed to notice.

He sank his hands in his jean's pockets. "Look, Cassie, I know you're reluctant to discuss what happened tonight, but the only way to stop this guy is to identify him."

Frustration welled inside, along with fear that crouched like a bobcat waiting to pounce. She leaned closer to Buck and placed her hand on his back.

"I don't have any useful information."

Her attacker had worn a mask and hadn't uttered a single word. Both encounters had been terrifying and mind-numbing. She'd been focused on escape, not taking mental notes of his person.

"You were engaged, right? To the guy who owns the co-op?"

"How did you find out?"

He frowned. "I noticed your reaction whenever you saw him at church. I was at the co-op buying supplies and spotted him, so I asked the cashier. She knew I worked for you. I guess that's why she felt compelled to give me your romantic history."

Her cheeks burned. She wondered how many details the cashier had shared with Luke. Did he know Brian ditched her because he lost interest? That he'd found Cassie boring? Or that he'd become enamored with a mutual friend?

"I forgot how long people's memories can be," she muttered.

The whole ordeal had been excruciating. For weeks, everyone in town had talked about the broken engagement. She'd grown weary of the pitying looks and well-intentioned pep talks. Just when she'd thought her broken heart had healed, Brian had started dating Valerie. Not only did that restart the gossip, it had hurt to see him and his new love around town. They were married now and expecting their first child. The sting of loss had disappeared, but the humiliation associated with the break-up remained.

"Could he have some sort of grudge against you?"

"Brian left me. If anyone has a right to be angry, it's me."

His brow furrowed. "What about other guys?"

Humiliation burned behind her sternum. "I haven't had a single date since Brian."

"How long ago was that?"

"Two years and three months."

"For what it's worth, he lost out on a good thing."

"That's sweet of you to say." Her discomfort at an all-time high, she unclipped Buck's ties and led him back into the stall.

"Has anyone invited you on a date, and you rejected them? Or someone who's hinted their interest?"

"There have been a few."

"We need to give their names to Detective Kane."

"I don't want to get anyone in trouble."

"The first step can be done without their knowledge. Kane will find out if any of them have violent offenses."

Closing the stall door, she yawned.

"Ready to call it a night?" Luke asked.

As much as she dreaded lying in bed and allowing the memories to crowd in, she couldn't put it off forever. "I'm glad the Lord brought you here, Luke."

He looked surprised. "I'm glad, too."

Luke's decision to come to Tulip hadn't been well thought out. Following his partner Simon's death and Luke's hospitalization, he'd had nothing to do between physical therapy sessions other than dwell on what had happened. His parents and friends had checked in on him often. They all said the same thing—Simon's death wasn't his fault, and he wouldn't want Luke to blame himself. His superior had ordered him to see a counselor, who then recommended Luke take extra time away from the job.

That had been the last straw. After many sleepless nights, he'd packed his gear, locked up the house and hit the road without telling a soul where he was going. It wasn't until two days later, when he'd received a frantic call from his mom that he'd revealed his destination. She'd expressed her reservations about the wisdom of his decision. Wes Wilder had turned her away before Luke was born, and she worried the Wilder children would be as callous and hurtful as their late father. He'd apologized for not telling her of his plans and reassured her that he'd be careful.

"More popcorn?"

He dragged his gaze from the television screen. Seated beside him with a thick blanket tucked around her lap, Cassie held a large bowl. She'd added peanut butter chocolate candies to the popcorn. Dusty was sprawled on his back on her other side, his belly exposed and his paws curled into the air.

When he'd hatched his plan to investigate his half siblings, he hadn't anticipated getting to know anyone else in Tulip.

"I've had my fill, thanks."

She popped another handful in her mouth. After he'd cleared the main house and pronounced it secure, she'd lingered in the kitchen, obviously reluctant to go to bed. He'd offered to watch television with her, and she'd eagerly accepted.

"Look at the dolphins." Pointing to the screen, she smiled, her eyes sparkling.

"I thought you'd choose a romantic comedy, not a documentary about sea life."

"I wanted to be a marine biologist at one time."

"Really?"

"We didn't take many vacations, which made each one a treat. My favorite was a beach trip when I got to swim with dolphins."

"How did you go from that to teaching?"

"In the end, I couldn't leave my parents or my hometown."

"You've never imagined living anywhere else? Lots of people can't wait to leave small towns."

"Spoken like a true rolling stone. I did live in Starkville when I attended Mississippi State. I enjoyed myself, but I always knew I wanted to live in Tulip and raise my future kids here." She cocked her head to one side. "Can you see yourself settling down someday? Putting down roots?"

Luke's throat constricted. Although he hadn't outright lied to Cassie, he was leading her to believe falsehoods. He had a life in Texas.

"I want to get married someday and have a couple of kids, if it's in God's plan."

"Kind of hard to have a serious relationship if you're bouncing from town to town."

"True."

Luke wanted to end the conversation. If he decided to walk away from this town without revealing the truth, he'd leave with no one the wiser. They'd forget about him in time. If, on the other hand, he decided not to ignore his heritage, everyone would know he'd come here under false pretenses. He should've thought this through, but he hadn't. He'd been desperate to escape the memories and the guilt, the knowledge that if not for him, Simon would be retired by now, soaking up the sun on a beach with his wife of forty-five years and looking forward to the birth of his first grandson.

He studied Cassie's profile. No, he hadn't realized he'd get to know anyone, let alone come to *like* anyone. While he was certain he'd leave Tulip one day, he didn't want to leave on bad terms.

She intercepted his gaze, her brows drawing together. "I'm keeping you up. It's almost midnight." She pushed aside the blanket and carried the bowl to the kitchen.

He twisted on the couch in order to see her better. "I'll stay up all night if that's what you need."

Cassie considered him. "I'm not paying you to baby-sit me."

"I've been through rough situations, and I know what it's

like to dread being alone with your thoughts. I was blessed with friends who dropped everything to be by my side."

He'd cracked open the door to his past with that statement, and he could see she wanted to kick it all the way open. Before he could anticipate her questions or how he might answer them, beams of light swept through the living room windows, followed by the crunch of tires on gravel right outside the house.

Dusty erupted into furious barking and leapt from the couch. Luke grabbed his gun from the side table and pushed the mute button on the TV remote. After turning off the living room lamps, he positioned himself at the windows overlooking the front porch and yard. The SUV's lights dimmed, and two figures exited, making no effort to mask their arrival. He reached over and flicked on the porch light.

"Who is it?" Cassie demanded.

He reengaged the gun safety. "Remi and Skye."

"At this time of night?"

She ordered Dusty to be silent, opened the door and propped it open. Cool air snuck in and wound around Luke.

"What's going on? Are Nash and Eden okay?"

"They're fine." Remi entered first, her astute gaze taking in the scene that must've looked like a cozy date night in. Noticing the gun at Luke's side, she frowned.

"We're sorry for showing up unannounced," Skye stated, traipsing in behind her future sister-in-law. The willowy, black-haired, green-eyed woman may not be a deputy any longer, but she hadn't lost the official air of law enforcement. "We didn't want to text in case you were already asleep."

Cassie glanced at the TV, the abandoned blanket, and his socks peeking from beneath his jeans. Her cheeks turned pink. "What brings you here?"

"Detective Kane reached out to me." Remi pulled off

her gloves and shoved them in her jacket pocket. "He told me what happened at the speech event. We came to see if you're all right." Her unspoken question weighed heavily in the room.

"I was planning to tell you tomorrow." Sighing, Cassie walked around the couch and sank onto the cushion. Dusty resumed his spot beside her, nudging her hand until she stroked his ears.

Remi and Skye sat on the love seat facing the windows. Luke remained where he was, debating when to make his exit. The women clearly weren't at complete ease around him.

They exchanged a glance that knotted his stomach. "You've learned something, haven't you?" he said.

"What is it?" Cassie's hand stilled on Dusty's head.

"Detective Kane is currently at another crime scene. He asked me to come and relay a troubling development." Remi took a deep breath. "At approximately 2100 hours, a woman was found murdered three blocks from where you were attacked."

Cassie pressed a hand to her mouth. That was maybe two hours after her attack.

Luke circled to the other side of the sofa and resumed his seat beside her. "Manner of death?"

"She was strangled." She grimaced. "That's not the worst part. The victim, Hana Moody, is about your height, with blond hair and brown eyes. She could be mistaken for you from a distance."

Luke watched the blood drain from Cassie's face.

"Are you saying an innocent woman died because I got away?"

FIVE

Luke's mind immediately went to serial killer. He just as quickly dismissed the notion. Serial killers weren't as common as people thought. What were the chances one would be living in small town Mississippi? But a good detective didn't discount possibilities until he had all the facts. While it was highly unlikely, it wasn't impossible.

He clasped her hand. "You're not at fault here. The victim's resemblance to you could be a fluke. There could be no connection whatsoever."

Cassie's gaze clung to his, tormented yet hopeful.

"We won't know until the crime scene investigators gather evidence and make their conclusions." Remi noticed their joined hands and frowned. Her gaze punched him with unspoken questions. What was his game? Did he have honorable intentions?

"I'd have caught this case if I'd been on shift tonight," she added regretfully. "I'd be the one in charge of catching this guy."

Skye shook her head, her glossy curls skimming her olive-green jacket. "You wouldn't be allowed to investigate because of your close connection to Cassie."

"Is Kane up to the task?" Luke asked.

Her hesitation was telling. "He's been on the job a long

time. I'm new at MPD, but I've heard he has a lot of experience."

Luke wondered what it was she wasn't saying.

"Cassie, why don't you stay at our place for a while?" Remi said.

Gauging her shell-shocked expression, he expected her to agree.

"I'm staying put."

"You're welcome any time. Our home is yours, you know."

"I know," she said softly, "and I appreciate it."

Skye stood up. "We'll touch base with you tomorrow."

Cassie accompanied Skye out onto the porch. Remi was almost to the door when she did an about-face.

"Cassie's not only my best friend, she's family. Don't hurt her."

If Remi knew he was law enforcement, she'd understand his commitment to Cassie's welfare.

He stood up. "You can trust me to watch out for her best interests. She gave me a job when I needed it, and she's been nothing but kind to me. I'm happy to do this for her."

Her eyes narrowed. "I'm not just talking about her physical safety. She's got this habit of seeing only the good in people."

"You don't believe she's capable of drawing her own conclusions?"

"I didn't say that. It's just she doesn't always accept that others might not have honorable motives."

"I'm not interested in romance, if that's what you're hinting at."

She searched his face. "Glad to hear it."

While Luke was slightly annoyed at her insinuations, he couldn't help but admire Remi Wilder's straight talk. The more he interacted with his half siblings, the more he wanted to learn about them. He'd heard through the Tulip grapevine that Remi had moved to Atlanta to be near her fiancé and that she'd returned after things soured between them.

After they left, Cassie put away the leftover popcorn while he let Dusty out one last time to do his business. She waited for her dog to follow her to bed. Her exhaustion was palpable.

"Thanks for staying up with me. You've gone above and beyond, and I appreciate it."

Guilt pierced him. He was torn between the desire to return to Texas—and leave the nagging feeling of wrong-doing behind—and staying in Tulip. "I'm happy to help in any way I can."

Her mouth quirked. "I think you deserve a raise."

"Good night, Cassie."

"Good night, Luke."

He retired to the guest bedroom. Unsurprisingly, he slept fitfully, worry about another invasion attempt mingling with his ever-growing guilt. He didn't wake her the following morning. On this particular Saturday, she didn't have any FFA or school-related tasks on her schedule.

He was finished with the chores and nursing his third cup of coffee when she finally emerged from her parents' bedroom. She looked cozy in her pink hoodie, black sweats and fuzzy socks. Her straight blond hair was tousled, her brown eyes sleepy, and there was a pillow crease in her pink cheek. Her face was devoid of makeup, and her mouth looked soft and inviting.

He had the surprising desire to test its softness. Would she welcome his kiss? His mouth went dry thinking about it. She was a beautiful woman—the sweetest he'd ever known, in fact.

"Sorry I overslept. Why didn't you wake me?" Her voice was husky.

"You needed the sleep."

"You're too good to me." She smiled sweetly, and he turned away to stare out the window.

She wouldn't look at him like that if she knew the true reason he was working on her ranch. He heard her moving around in the kitchen, pouring coffee and retrieving creamer from the fridge. He'd seen several seasonal flavors in there, all too sweet for him.

"What's on the agenda for today?"

He turned to the kitchen. "I forgot to get corn and oats at the co-op yesterday, so I'll have to make another trip."

After stirring in the creamer and testing her coffee, she dropped the spoon in the sink. "I'll come with you. I need to look at the boots." She took a long sip. "I probably need to grab a few groceries, too, if you have time."

"I'm in no rush. When we get back, I'll distribute the salt blocks in the pastures. I wanted to run something by you about the chicken house. It takes a solid day to clean it out. My uncle put down rubber mats and created a sort of litter-box situation at his place. It cut the clean-out to an hour."

"That's a good idea. How much would it cost?"

"I can price the rubber mats today. As for the litter box, I saw some old gate sections on the ranch we could use for the hens to sit on."

"I like your suggestion. Anything to make ranch work easier is a good thing." She entered the living room. "Does your uncle live nearby?"

He nodded. "He has a farm about twenty minutes away from my parents' place. I started working for him when I was fourteen. Part time during the school year and full time during summers."

"Did your sister help out, too?"

He laughed. "Paige likes animals, but she doesn't like the mess that goes along with them. She preferred to work at the neighborhood pizza parlor where she could flirt with boys and get good tips."

"Smart girl." She smiled.

"What do your mom and dad do?"

"My mom's a school librarian. Dad is a pediatric dentist."

She brought the mug to her lips. "How come you didn't stay and work on your uncle's farm?"

Before the attacks on Cassie, he'd kept their interactions brief—for just this reason. He was determined not to outright lie to her.

Oh, like lies of omission or allowing someone to believe untruths is somehow better?

When he'd kept Cassie at a distance, he'd managed to avoid these conversations. The web he'd woven was beginning to entangle him.

"Why stay in Texas when there's a whole country to explore?" He downed the remainder of his coffee, washed out the cup and headed for the door. "I forgot something in the apartment. When do you want to leave?"

"Um, half an hour?"

Luke escaped to the loft, the Bible on his nightstand a stark reminder of his faith and values. *I'm sorry, God. I know my interests are self-serving, and I know the right thing to do. But I can't come clean to Cassie yet. I'm not ready. Plus, she has more important matters to deal with right now.*

Luke was relieved when Cassie didn't resume her questions on the ride to town. She was quiet, her brows drawn together as she contemplated the winter landscape rolling past. At the co-op, she insisted she didn't need him to stay with her. There were plenty of shoppers, so he agreed to separate.

Luke quickly made his way to the other building and loaded the supplies onto a platform cart. When he returned to the clothing section, he saw Cassie speaking with a heavily pregnant brunette near the boots display. He saw past Cassie's polite smile to the strain around her eyes and the white-knuckle grip on her crossbody bag.

Out of the corner of his eye, he noticed a dark-headed, bearded man approaching the pair. Brian Swartz, the man who'd made Cassie the center of Tulip's gossip mill. Brian linked hands with the brunette and smiled tightly at Cassie.

Luke abandoned the cart and strode between the racks. Reaching Cassie's side, he draped his arm around her shoulders. She looked up at him in surprise.

"I'm starving," Luke drawled. "How about I treat you to lunch over at the Pit Stop? I'll even throw in that cobbler you like so much."

Cassie momentarily lost her voice. Luke hadn't ever been this close or familiar. Tucked beneath his arm, she could feel the hardened muscle over his ribs. His woodsy scent beckoned her closer. His crystal-blue eyes, framed by intelligent black brows and thick lashes, had the power to melt her bones. Her gaze dipped to his mouth, and her stomach did a somersault.

Brian cleared his throat, reminding her of their audience.

"I could go for some cobbler," she said breathlessly.

He flashed that pulse-pounding grin, and for a moment, Cassie wished he wasn't just her employee.

"I don't think we've officially met," Valerie stated.

Cassie dragged her gaze to the other couple. Valerie was rubbing her extended stomach, her gaze fixated on Luke. Brian wore a dark scowl. Beyond Brian's shoulder, she could see Mr. and Mrs. Ruffalo slowly pushing their cart, staring and whispering. A timely reminder why romance was such a huge risk in this town. If she fell for Luke and he left, everyone would pity her again. Besides, how could she ever hope to hold a cowboy's interest if she couldn't make Brian happy?

When Cassie didn't make introductions, Luke held out his free hand.

"I'm Luke Fisher."

"I'm Valerie. This is my husband, Brian."

"Nice to meet you both." He lightly squeezed Cassie's shoulder. "Cassie and I have to run. You all have a great day."

He steered her to the cart in the aisle, not releasing her until they reached the cash registers. Once their purchases were loaded, they climbed into his truck.

She finally found her voice. "How did you know?"

He started the engine. "You looked uncomfortable. When I noticed him approaching, I decided to intervene. Do you mind?"

"Um, no." She lifted her crossbody purse over her head and placed it on the seat between them. "Have you always been observant?"

"I suppose so." He glanced through the rearview window as he backed out of the space. "I was serious about lunch. I've become fond of the Pit Stop's meatloaf and mashed potatoes."

"I'm partial to the chicken pot pie. Since I'm so busy with school and FFA, I eat a lot of my meals at my parents'. My mom happens to dislike chicken pot pie, so the café is my go-to when I'm craving it."

The café was bustling. The only open booth overlooked the street and was close to the entrance. This made it convenient for folks to stop on their way in or out. While she appreciated their concern, the constant questions about the case—none of which she could answer—killed her appetite and ramped up her anxiety. By the time their meal arrived, she could barely swallow.

Luke's eyes flashed an apology. "This was a bad idea." He waved his fork toward her untouched plate. "Why don't we take this to go?"

"That would probably be best."

She took a sip of Sprite, and the bubbles coated her throat. Luke glanced around, likely searching for Penny, their waitress. His brows tugged together.

"Who's the guy at the counter?"

She looked over her shoulder. Every seat was filled, and most of them were men eating alone. "Which one?"

"Red track suit. That's your high school emblem, right? Does he work at the school?"

Cassie homed in on the man in question. Seated at the far end near the swinging kitchen door, he had close-cropped dirty-blond hair, a square jaw and wide-set blue eyes. Intercepting his gaze, she offered a polite smile and wave.

"That's Jim Hallman. He's the gym teacher."

"He can't seem to stop staring at you."

"I'm sure everyone in this place is staring."

He ran his thumb over his mug handle. "Has he ever asked you out?"

"Jim's married. His wife, Tracy, doesn't get out much. She's a homebody."

"He's never set off red flags?"

"Jim and I don't often interact. He stays in his athletic lane, and I stay in my ag lane. There's not a lot of overlap, even in a school as small as ours. He's polite when we do cross paths."

Luke's mouth tightened. "He's headed this way."

"Hi, Cassie. I'm sorry to interrupt your meal. I thought you might want to see this." He placed a newspaper on the corner of the table. "It's the *Mayfield Herald*."

Foreboding skated over her skin. Unfolding the thick paper, she found herself staring at a photograph of a young woman who could be her sibling. This was the murder victim Remi and Skye had told them about. The brief article stated that Hana Moody was a dance instructor and had been murdered near her studio.

She rubbed her sternum, where a burning sensation had become lodged.

Luke pushed his plate aside. "Can I see that?"

She handed him the paper and watched his features harden as he skimmed the information.

Jim fiddled with the zipper on his red jacket. "There's no mention of any suspects. Have you heard if the police have anyone in mind?"

Cassie shook her head. "I haven't heard anything."

"What about witnesses?" Jim pressed.

"We don't know any more than you do," Luke said, his voice uncompromising. "Do you mind if I keep this?"

"Not at all." Jim stared at Cassie. "Take care of yourself."

Cassie barely acknowledged his departure because her thoughts were spinning.

The burning sensation spread in her chest. "Do you think he chose her on purpose? Because she looked like me?"

"I don't have enough information to give you a good answer," Luke said. "In my mind, this was a crime of opportunity. There wasn't enough time for him to scout out a victim who matched your description."

Luke's viewpoint made sense to her, and Cassie latched onto it wholeheartedly. She hoped he was right. It would mean the man after her wasn't willing to take an innocent woman's life just because he couldn't get her.

SIX

Once they were in Luke's truck, the to-go boxes on the seat between them, she turned to him. "I normally enjoy my free Saturdays, but right now, having time on my hands is a bad thing. I thought about what you said about the chicken house. Did you happen to price the rubber mats?"

He shoved his seat belt into its slot and outlined the cost investment.

"Let's go back to the co-op. I can get groceries tomorrow after church."

Back at the ranch, they worked together to remove the existing boxes and scrape the floor clean of debris. After they laid down the rubber mats, Luke brought in a pair of discarded gates and rigged a homemade litter box on either side. The project ate up the afternoon. They worked well together. The more time she spent in Luke's company, the more she craved it.

"This is going to make cleanup much easier," she said, dusting her hands on her jeans. "I'm glad you suggested it."

He chugged the contents of his water bottle and flashed a tired but satisfied grin. Her pulse skipped in response. His disheveled hair was damp at the temples and had fallen onto his forehead. There was a slight shadow of a beard along his jaw. He'd pushed up the sleeves of his Henley, revealing muscular forearms sprinkled with dark hair.

Her phone sounded an alert. Pulling it from her back pocket, she read the text. "Remi wants me to meet her at Skye's. We'll eat supper and go over some wedding stuff."

"You should go."

Cassie felt a pinch of disappointment. She'd envisioned another evening watching television with Luke.

He closed the outer door and locked it. "Where does she live?"

"Skye has a camper that's parked on a friend's property. It's fifteen minutes from here."

"I'll drop you off if you don't want to drive alone."

Cassie was tempted to take him up on the offer, but she had to stop depending on him. His presence here was fleeting. He could be gone tomorrow.

When she declined, he asked her to text him when she got to Skye's.

During the brief drive through the dwindling daylight, anxiety reared its ugly head. She half expected her attacker to suddenly appear on the road ahead. She wondered where he was at that moment. Plotting another attack on her or someone else?

God, I ask that You comfort Hana Moody's family. Please guide the police to this man who needs to be locked up for his crimes.

At Skye's, she sidestepped talk of her situation and strove to keep the conversation on the upcoming nuptials. The evening with her friends helped ease her troubled spirit. Remi's truck behind her on the road home gave a modicum of comfort. Being friends with Remi and Skye—a police detective and former deputy—had its perks. Nash was former military. Luke was proving to be a brave and cool-headed protector. She would have to ask him if he'd also served in the military.

Her truck bounced lightly over the packed gravel drive.

The porch light was a beacon in the darkness. Luke opened the door and stepped onto the porch to wait for her. Dusty streaked past him and bounded down the stairs, jumping in excitement until she exited the truck.

"How did it go?"

"Good." She climbed the stairs, physical and mental fatigue overtaking her. "I'm glad I went. Thanks for keeping me busy today."

He shrugged. "You are the boss. You want a revamped chicken coop, that's what you get."

There it was again—the reminder that their relationship was a professional one. He was careful to make that distinction. The last couple of days had pushed them into friendly territory. Did he worry she wanted more from him? While Cassie thought he was the most handsome, most intriguing man she'd ever met, she would keep that information to herself. Luke was proving to be insightful, though. Maybe he'd sensed the interest she'd tried to bury?

With that in mind, she bid him goodnight and escaped to her parents' bedroom. She wasn't about to push her company onto any man, much less one who was earning a paycheck on her ranch.

Sunday was another day of trying to keep herself busy while waiting impatiently for an update from Detective Kane. Church was both a blessing and a trial, with folks smothering her with their concern. After the service, she rode home with Remi, leaving Luke to drive back to her ranch alone. She didn't return home until late, and she didn't linger in the living room with him once she returned home.

After school Monday, she had supper in Arianna's office. It was parent-teacher conference night, and there wouldn't be time to go home and back before the meetings commenced.

"Evan's getting impatient for an answer to his proposal,"

Arianna said, stabbing a tomato with her fork. "I don't know what to tell him. I don't want to lose him, but I'm not sure I'm ready for marriage."

Seated behind her desk, the florescent lights glinted in her upswept red hair. The window blinds were open, offering a view of the darkened parking lot and circles of light cast by the utility poles.

Cassie took another bite of her ham and cheese sandwich. Picking up the framed photo of Arianna and Evan, she studied the couple. Arianna was in one of her signature pant suits. This one was an emerald color that matched her eyes and complemented her creamy complexion. Her nails were always painted and her jewelry was bold and sparkly. Dark-headed, brown-eyed Evan was wearing a polo, jeans and tennis shoes. Despite their different styles and approaches to life, the couple complemented each other.

Six years older than Cassie, veterinarian Evan had moved to Tulip and joined the vet office while she was attending Mississippi State. The single dad didn't talk about his first wife. His daughter, Morgan, had volunteered that Georgia Tucker had hit the road and never looked back. After two years together, Arianna and Evan's fondness for each other was obvious. It helped that Arianna and Morgan had hit it off.

"He adores you," Cassie said. "Of course he's worried. How long ago did he propose?"

Arianna took a sip of her flavored seltzer water and grimaced. "A week and a half."

"You told him about your past." Arianna had been left at the altar—literally. At least Brian had canceled his and Cassie's wedding three months prior to their wedding date.

"He thinks I don't trust him."

"He's been hurt, too. He needs to try to understand your perspective."

Arianna pushed her salad aside and rested her chin on her hand. "I hate that I'm making him unhappy."

"Don't let him pressure you, though."

This wasn't the first time they'd had this conversation, and Cassie was concerned Arianna might cave to Evan's cajoling and have regrets later.

There was a knock on the door, and Gabriela poked her head in. "Cassie, your first appointment is here early. I directed them to your classroom."

"Thanks, Gabriela." She slid her leftover sandwich into the bag and fished a breath mint from her bag. "See you later, A."

After greeting her first set of parents, she got down to business. The meetings were back-to-back, some of them more pleasant than others. Most of her students were applying themselves and earning good marks. There were several who needed to focus more on schoolwork and less on their social lives, however. After the last parents left, Cassie began to pack her things. The school was quiet, and she wondered how many teachers were left in the building. In her haste to leave, she knocked over her soda can. Liquid splashed onto her desk calendar. Hurrying into her supply closet, which was outfitted with a sink, she grabbed a fistful of paper towels. When she exited and noticed a figure blocking the doorway, she yelped.

"I didn't mean to startle you," Luke said, holding his Stetson in both hands.

"Luke. What are you doing here?"

"I texted and asked when you were leaving. When I didn't get a response and no answer to my call, I got worried."

Cassie blew out a breath. "I forgot to tell you I'd have my phone on silent during our parent meetings. Thanks for checking on me."

He opened his mouth to speak. If he said anything about

their boss-employee relationship, she just might scream. Before he could answer her, the building was plunged into darkness.

"Luke?" Cassie's voice wobbled.

"I'm here." He activated his phone light. "Any idea how many people are left in the building?"

Cassie crossed from her desk to the doorway. "I don't know. Gabriela is the last one to leave on conference nights. Elias, our maintenance man, locks up behind her."

The hallway was pitch black. "I came in through the front. Gabriela was near the flagpole speaking with a couple. I didn't see anyone in the main entrance hall, and the class-rooms in this wing were empty." He moved to the nearby exit door. "Let's go outside and around to the parking lot."

He pushed on the lever, but the door wouldn't budge.

Cassie tried the other door. "I haven't seen Elias tonight. This shouldn't be locked."

Shining the light through the slim window slat, he peered through it and saw metal chairs wedged beneath the han-dles—confirmation that this was a deliberate act.

At his hesitation, Cassie peered over his shoulder. The air seemed to leak out of her.

"Any chance this is a student prank?" he asked.

"Doubtful. Those are left for the last week of school be-fore graduation. I'm going to call the police." In the glare of her phone screen, he saw her frown. "I don't have ser-vice. Do you?"

He checked his phone, his gut hardening. "No. Whoever's behind this must be using a signal jammer."

"My attacker hasn't given up, has he?"

A scream echoed down the corridor, and Cassie grabbed his wrist. He wove his fingers through hers. "We stay to-gether."

She nodded, her eyes huge. They passed the deserted

classrooms one after another. As they neared the library and principal's office, a flickering orange glow ate up the darkness.

"I smell smoke," Cassie whispered.

Luke's steps faltered. He tightened his grip on her hand, his mind and body rebelling.

"Luke, something's on fire."

The smell sent him straight back to the late summer night that had changed him forever. The event that left him questioning if he wanted to stay in law enforcement. Locked in a garage and left to burn, he and Simon had tried everything possible to find a way out. Luke had broken a finger pounding on the door. When the paramedics arrived on scene, they'd remarked on his broken fingernails and bloodied palms.

Cassie touched his chest. "What's wrong?"

He shifted his gaze to her frightened, confused face.

Lord, please help me. I don't want to let her down, too.

"This way." He picked up the pace.

Rounding the corner, he counted several barrels. The contents had been lit. He recoiled.

"I see Gabriela!" Cassie exclaimed.

The principal and several others rushed up to the doors and tried to get them open to help Luke and Cassie out.

"See those chains?" Luke pointed. "He made sure no one was getting in that way."

Grabbing an extinguisher affixed to the wall outside the cafeteria, he put out the flames.

"Help! Someone help me!"

The cry came from inside the cafeteria. Cassie sprinted over and dashed inside without a thought to who was waiting on the other side. Luke unholstered his weapon and followed right behind her.

She crouched beside a long table where a woman sat clutching her ankle. "Freya, what happened?"

"I had finished the pantry inventory and was about to leave when a man busted in and barreled into me." Tears streamed down her face. Her uniform and name badge told him she was the kitchen manager. "I tripped over that chair and fell. My ankle's killing me. It's already swelling. I don't think I can put weight on it."

"Where did he go?" Luke asked.

"I'm not sure."

"Did you see his face?"

She shook her head. "He was wearing a mask."

"We'll help you." Cassie looped an arm around Freya.

Luke shoved his weapon back in its holster and moved to her other side. When they got her to her feet, she cried out in pain and lifted her injured foot off the floor.

"Easy," Luke instructed. "Lean on me. Cassie, can you check those doors to the courtyard?"

Using her phone's flashlight to light the way, she ran between the tables and jostled each one. "Locked."

"There's an exit in the back of the kitchen," Freya volunteered. "The cafeteria staff uses it."

"I'll go." Cassie started toward the kitchen.

"What happened to staying together?" Luke didn't want her out of his sight even for a minute. While the going would be slow due to Freya's injury, it was safer to stay in a group.

Cassie waited on them and held the kitchen door. Her light swept over the stainless-steel counters and equipment, sinks and drink station. They progressed deeper into the space, passing the professional dish washer machine and upright freezers. A couple of garbage cans were gathered near the exit.

"Let's hope he didn't get to this one," Cassie murmured. She turned the lock, twisted the knob and pushed the door open. Fresh, brisk air seeped inside. "Thank You, Lord," she breathed.

Luke added his own silent prayer of thanks as he assisted Freya, who leaned on him heavily and hopped on her good foot. They exited into the courtyard. He squinted into the night, unable to separate the shapes of tables and trees from the shadows.

Freya leaned against the brick and caught her breath. Luke was about to turn and speak to Cassie when the door slammed shut.

Whirling, he stared at the painted brown metal barrier. Cassie wasn't right behind him like he thought. She was on the other side of that door, alone in the kitchen.

No, not alone.

His blood ran cold. Lunging for the knob, he heard the lock engage. He pounded on the door. "Cassie!"

Her muffled scream injected terror into his veins.

SEVEN

Her attacker seemed to come out of nowhere. Luke's desperation leaked through the locked door. He couldn't help her, and the man who wanted her dead knew it. His arm around her waist, he spun her around, letting go mid-spin so that she lost her balance and crashed to the floor. Her head connected with the dishwasher, and her right elbow hit the tile hard. Ignoring the pain, Cassie rolled out of reach, got onto her hands and knees and crawled toward the front part of the kitchen. If she could get a head start, she could make her way to the auditorium or gymnasium and possibly find an exit he hadn't sabotaged.

He snagged her collar, yanking hard enough that her top buttons dug into her throat. She kicked back and out, somehow catching him in the knee with her boot. His yowl pierced her eardrums. Cassie took advantage of his momentary distraction, clambered to her feet, and stumbled past the freezers.

He overtook her, his palms landing in the middle of her back and shoving her forcefully into the counter. The hard metal edge jammed into her ribs. Bands of pain circled outward. He seized a fistful of her hair and yanked her back against his chest. She used both elbows as weapons and managed to dislodge him.

The faint glow of an exit sign shone on a set of knives. She swept her arm out, her fingertips snagging the tip of a handle. Just as his arm came around her midsection again, she slid the knife from its slot and brought her hand down, jabbing at his leg. He anticipated her intent and sprang out of the way. She tried again. This time, he captured her wrist and slammed it against the counter, forcing her fingers to release the knife.

A shuddering crash, followed by shattering glass, startled them both. His head whipped up, and she got a glimpse of his eyes. Dark brown possibly, but not blue or green.

"Cassie!" Luke's voice boomed into the space.

With a hiss of impatience, the man started to retreat. He probably planned to take the same exit Luke and Freya had used. Cassie couldn't let him get away again. Ignoring the fear threatening to freeze her in place, she tackled him.

Luke stepped through the jagged hole in the cafeteria window, pistol armed and ready, and homed in on the sounds of struggle. He hurried into the kitchen at the same time a masked man untangled himself from Cassie.

"Stop right there or you'll get a bullet hole in your chest," Luke warned.

The man hesitated for a split second before diving low, ramming into Luke's legs and propelling him backward. He landed two blows to Luke's torso. The third was a direct hit to his weak shoulder. Red-hot pain streaked into his arm, upper shoulder and neck. The momentary distraction cost him. The man shoved past him and ran out into the cafeteria.

Cassie climbed to her feet. He couldn't make out much more than her shape in the blacked-out building.

"Are you hurt?" he demanded.

"I'm fine."

Satisfied she was okay, he pursued his quarry through the cafeteria, into the hallway and toward the auditorium. At the last second, he veered right. Luke changed course as well, following him into the gym. He debated whether to discharge his weapon and decided against it. There was no way of knowing if any of the teachers or parents had sought cover in this wing of the school. He couldn't risk a stray bullet hitting an innocent civilian.

Their shoes pounding against the polished floor echoed in the massive space. He was closing in on his prey. A few more strides, and he'd have him.

Metal clanged against the floor. Basketballs bounced and rolled. Another crash. More basketballs. As he navigated the obstacles in the near darkness, a door slammed open and closed. Yells erupted in the locker rooms.

Luke slowed long enough to remove his phone and activate the flashlight. Easing into the space with his light in one hand and gun in the other, he discovered three teen boys huddled beneath the sinks. Their eyes were wide with terror.

"Where'd he go?"

The biggest one pointed Luke toward the rear of the room.

He pushed through the door with enough force to crash it into the wall. Lungs heaving, his shoulder aching, he saw nothing but the darkened football stadium in the distance. The grass provided a cushion for the attacker's shoes, masking his escape route.

Slamming his fist into the door, Luke returned to the locker room and escorted the frightened students to the cafeteria. He found Cassie in the courtyard with Freya, Gabriela and several couples.

"He got away," he told them. "Found these three in the locker room."

Once again, the biggest one spoke for the group. "Coach

said the school would be open tonight and that we could get some extra practice in. Then the lights went out. When we heard screaming, we hid."

The one with glasses spoke up. "I want to go home."

Putting his weapon away, Luke held up his hand. "No one goes home yet. We have to give statements to the police."

"They should be on their way," Gabriela stated, her face grave. "One of the parents got in his vehicle and drove away from the school in search of a cell signal. Do we know if there are others hiding in the building?"

"I checked each classroom in the gymnasium wing," Luke replied. "If there are people still inside, they didn't respond to my summons."

Cassie cradled her ribs. "Has anyone seen Elias?"

Gabriela's brow furrowed. "We have to locate him."

Luke wondered if the janitor had come across the attacker. He could be hurt and unable to seek assistance. "I'll search for him."

Cassie grasped his arm. "I'll go with you."

Before he could respond, the lights came back on. Gasps and murmurs filtered through the group. Yellow light spilled through the oversize windows. Luke turned to Cassie, relieved to finally see her fully.

Her lower lip was busted. There was a nasty abrasion near her hairline. Her arms and hands were scraped up, too. When that door had slammed shut, trapping her with her attacker, Luke had been on the verge of panic.

Taking her hand, he led her away from the group. "What happened after he got you alone?"

"We struggled. I fought as hard as I could. I tried to stab him, but I don't think I got him."

Registering movement out of the corner of his eye, Luke pivoted toward a man stepping through the open window.

"Elias! Where were you?" Gabriela went to meet him. "Are you hurt?"

"No, ma'am. I sought refuge in the custodial closet." He rubbed a hand over his buzzed black hair. Probably in his late fifties, he was about the same height as Luke and physically fit. "But then I thought I'd better try and get the lights on. I discovered the main electrical switch had been tripped."

Sheriff Hines and two of his deputies arrived, along with a fire truck and ambulance. Freya had the worst injury and was checked out first. The interviews took a while. Luke finished before Cassie, and he headed to his truck to wait for her. He pulled out his phone, relieved the jammer had been found and switched off.

He dialed the number of a buddy and coworker. Cameron Hersh answered on the third ring.

"You'd better be calling to say you're reporting for work soon, McCoy."

"Hersh. How are you? How's Amber? Has she had the baby yet?"

"Come home and see for yourself."

He reached up to massage his shoulder. "It's not the right time."

Hersh's sigh was resigned. "Amber's good. She has three more weeks to go before little Mia gets here."

"Tell her I'm praying for her and Mia."

"I will. Listen, McCoy, we need you. The city needs you. And I'm guessing you need us."

The faces of Luke's fellow officers paraded through his mind, and he experienced a ping of longing—his first since the accident. He did miss the people he worked alongside and the satisfaction of putting criminals behind bars. But if he went back, Simon wouldn't be there. Luke would have a new partner. He wasn't sure he could handle that.

Hersh spoke into the ongoing silence. "Where are you? Your mom was cagey when I asked."

"Mississippi."

"What are you doing there?"

"Listen, Hersh, I called to ask a favor. I've encountered a bit of a situation here. Can you access the NCIC database and do a search for murder cases with specific victim bios? I'll send you the info. I'm interested in the southern Mississippi area."

"Asking questions at this point is useless, isn't it?"

"Someone I know is being targeted."

"Send me the info, and I'll get to work on it."

"I owe you one."

"You owe me a steak dinner."

Luke laughed, memories of the barbecues he'd hosted reminding him of the good times. Of course, Simon and his wife had been regulars.

He heard gravel dislodge behind him, and he jerked around to find Nash standing on the other side of his truck bed. His expression was serious, and his eyes were full of questions.

How much had he overheard?

EIGHT

"I've got to go."

"I'll be in touch," Hersh promised.

Luke tucked the phone into his pocket and draped his arms over the truck ledge. His shoulder didn't like that, so he straightened. "Did Cassie call you?"

"Remi's on duty tonight and heard what went down. She contacted me." Nash glanced at the school, his face reflecting his disquiet. "I spoke to Gabriela when I pulled in. She told me what you did."

"The suspect got away again."

"But Cassie, Freya and the others are safe," he countered, bringing his attention back to Luke.

His expression reflected respect and admiration, and Luke acknowledged he craved his brother's approval.

"You're being called a hero," Nash said.

He inwardly flinched. A hero didn't let his partner die. "I want this guy behind bars, where he can't pose a threat to Cassie or anyone else. You would've done the same thing. Remi and Skye, too, if they'd been in my place."

He cocked his head to one side. "Did you serve in the military?"

"No."

"My sister and fiancée have law enforcement training. Some might say you conduct yourself like a cop."

"Some might, that's true."

"Are you?"

Coming into this, Luke had been determined not to outright lie.

"I am a police officer."

Nash's jaw went slack.

Luke held up his hand. "I'm on medical leave, though, and I don't know when or even if I'll continue in law enforcement."

"I suppose you don't feel like sharing details."

"No, I don't."

"Does Cassie know?"

"You're the first person I've told, and only because you asked me point blank."

Would Nash share this information with Remi and Skye? Would he tell Cassie? Any one of them were likely to do a search on him. Frankly, he was surprised they hadn't done it before now. If they dug into the life of Luke Fisher, they wouldn't find information about him, and that would inspire a whole new set of questions.

"I don't know how you wound up in Tulip, but I'm grateful you've got Cassie's back."

"I'll do what I can to protect her."

He studied him for a long moment. "I believe you."

It seemed he'd earned Nash's trust with his revelation. Would he understand if Luke told him the whole truth? That they were brothers? Would he want to get to know Luke McCoy? Or, like Wes Wilder, would Nash reject him outright?

His phone beeped, and he relayed the text. "It's from Cassie. Detective Kane's on scene and wants to talk to me."

They walked around the building to the courtyard, which was crawling with deputies and Mayfield PD officers. Cassie was standing with the detective and waved them over.

Nash engulfed Cassie in a bear hug. Luke stood aside, strangely wishing he could be the one holding her.

When they parted, Cassie gestured to Kane. "This is Remi's brother, Nash."

"We've met before, although in better circumstances," Kane said, inclining his head. Once again, Kane looked as if he'd slept in his suit. "Mr. Fisher, I'd like for you and Miss West to walk me through the school and outline what went down."

Nash hung back while the three of them entered the cafeteria. Cassie led the way through the hallways to her classroom. Already, a crime scene investigator was checking the exit doors for prints. Inside the room, Kane extracted disposable gloves from his pocket and handed them each a pair. "In case you forget and touch something."

As they pulled on the gloves, Kane got his notepad and pen ready. "Tell me about the events leading up to the power outage."

Cassie's hands curled into tight balls. Jutting her chin, she relayed the information as concisely as possible. There was no denying the fear in her eyes, however. Luke admired her courage. Her sunny outlook and kindness made it easy to overlook her inner fortitude.

As they shared details about the fire, Luke's chest got tight. He would hate fire for the rest of his life. His unease must've been obvious, because Cassie slipped her hand into his and squeezed. He felt her warmth through the gloves. He looked down into her liquid brown eyes. Here she was attempting to comfort him, when she was the one who'd gone toe-to-toe with a murderer.

When they made their way back into the kitchen, they found more investigators scouring for evidence. He prayed there'd be a hair or blood sample that would identify their enemy.

Cassie accompanied him and Kane to the gym. The basketballs were haphazardly strewn across the polished gym floor. At the exit door, Kane crouched and scanned the ground for shoe imprints.

"The ground's too dry."

"How's the investigation into Hana Moody's death?" Cassie asked.

"I don't have anything new to share," he hedged.

Luke's gaze narrowed. "You found something, though."

Kane tugged on his already loosened tie.

Cassie looked between them. "Is he right?"

"We've run down a witness."

"That's wonderful," Cassie exclaimed. "Why didn't you tell me?"

"He's not what you'd consider credible."

"What does that mean?"

"He's a homeless man known to the department for abusing heroin."

"Did he give a description though?" She spread her hands. "Even if his word can't be used in court, you could search for the suspect, right?"

"I wish we could act on his account. Anyway, it wasn't very specific. He saw a man from a distance who pulled off a mask and shoved it in his jacket. He said the man was average height and lean. He didn't get any other details. I know it's disappointing, but we're going to keep working the case."

Cassie sighed. "Can you tell me if you found a belt at the scene?"

Kane's head reared back. "How did you know that? We haven't released that information."

"I mentioned the belt in my interview with you."

Luke's annoyance grew as Kane flipped through the pages of his notebook.

"I don't have that written down. You were in shock. It's understandable you'd get confused about what you did or didn't say."

She squared her shoulders. "Detective Kane, I specifically mentioned that he used a belt during the first attack at the school barn."

"I didn't have a record of it." Scribbling something down, he shoved the notebook back into his pocket. "Now I do."

Luke squashed the urge to give the man a review on the importance of police procedures. "Was it thin and black?"

"Yes."

Cassie inched closer to Luke. "Does that mean we have a serial killer in our midst?"

"I'm not ruling it out," Kane replied. "But I urge you to keep that information to yourselves. People tend to panic when they hear those words."

Without giving them a chance to respond, Kane stalked inside the building. Luke and Cassie stayed put.

He peeled off the disposable gloves and shoved them in his pocket.

"When I asked Remi if Kane could handle this case, I got the feeling she didn't have full confidence in his abilities. I'm beginning to share her opinion."

Her expression clouded. "What can we do? At this point, we don't have grounds to make a formal complaint. And I don't want to cause trouble for Remi."

"We pester him. Bombard him with calls, texts, in-person visits. Let him know we expect answers."

"I like that idea."

Luke reached up and traced the lower curve of her lip. "I'm sorry you got hurt."

Her sudden intake of air was loud in the night, and he

became aware of the intimacy of his touch. Her eyes were wide and questioning. Curling his fingers, he lowered his arm to his side.

"How are your ribs?" he asked, hoping to distract them both from the sudden awareness spiraling through the air.

"Bruised," she murmured. "Not broken."

"Good."

They continued to stare at each other, locked in some sort of limbo.

"Well." She licked her lips. "I suppose I should get my stuff from the classroom."

"Right."

He turned, waved her inside and closed the door behind them. What had he been thinking? What was she thinking?

Luke quickly silenced the questions. He couldn't let himself get distracted by her sweetness and beauty.

After Cassie collected her personal belongings, they said goodbye to Nash, and Luke walked Cassie to her vintage truck.

"I'll follow you home." He stowed her bulging backpack on the bench seat.

She lifted her crossbody bag over her head and put it with the backpack. Turning to him, she searched his face. "I couldn't help but notice your reaction to the fire."

He braced himself. In the initial phase of his employment, Cassie hadn't put him on the spot or poked into his private life. Things were changing between them, however, and she was becoming more interested in his thoughts and motivations. Or maybe she'd always been interested but had kept her curiosity contained.

"You froze," she said into the ensuing silence. "You went somewhere else in your mind, didn't you?"

He nodded, keeping his expression closed and hoping she would drop it.

"What's the significance, Luke? Why did it bother you so much?"

Memories of that dreadful night rushed in, and he closed his eyes. "I lost someone in a fire."

I lost someone in a fire.

Cassie couldn't let go of Luke's reluctant admission. Couldn't forget his pained, despondent expression. She'd tossed and turned the whole night through, her mind refusing to settle as it replayed this latest attack. Luke had gone into warrior mode from the onset of trouble, and she'd gained comfort just from having him by her side. When her attacker had separated her from Luke, she'd fought with all her strength, knowing he wouldn't rest until he found a way back to her side. He hadn't proven her wrong. He'd rescued her with no thought to his own safety.

Sitting astride Buck, she glanced over at him. He'd taken a shine to her fifteen-year-old black quarter horse, King, and he sat tall and limber in the saddle. The morning sun poured over him, washing him in gold and sparkling off the dew in the fields. His Stetson shaded his eyes, but she had a clear view of his straight nose, the curve of his mouth and the sculpted lines of his cheekbones and jaw. He hadn't gotten a haircut since he arrived, and his hair was starting to curl over his coat collar.

She pressed her lips together, the memory of the pads of his fingers brushing against her sensitive skin as sharp as if he'd touched her a minute ago. Her mouth dried at the thought of him actually kissing her. Cassie breathed in the bracing air.

Like it or not, her feelings for the enigmatic cowboy were growing and going somewhere that was probably unwise. Her desire to know more about him, to know *everything* about him, was deepening. Her respect for his privacy was becoming outmatched by this ever-demanding need. His obvious grief had kept her from pressing him last night. This morning, when she'd gotten the notification that classes were canceled, she'd started mulling over how to broach the subject again.

After they'd fed the chickens and pigs, Luke invited her to ride with him to inspect the fences. She'd readily accepted, even though fence checking was tedious work.

He pointed to a section with broken strands of barbed wire, dismounted and retrieved a small tool sack and a coil of smooth wire from his saddlebag. Cassie dismounted and joined him by the fence.

He deftly twisted a loop into each end of the broken strand. Doing the same with the new wire, he joined them together and used a wire tightener to pull it taut.

Cassie pointed to one of the metal posts. "T-clip has popped off." Snagging his flathead screwdriver, she installed a new clip.

Luke scooped up the tool sack and held it out for her to drop the screwdriver into. As he put it back into the saddle bag, he said, "Think your parents will come home soon?"

She gazed at the pond in the other pasture where a pair of ducks were taking their morning bath. "They want to be here, but my grandmother doesn't have anyone else to help her. She's not exactly thrilled about moving into an assisted living community. They're trying to help her adjust to the idea. They have to settle on a realtor to sell her house and arrange for an estate sale of her furniture and belongings. My mom sounded stressed when I spoke to her yesterday."

"The school attack isn't going to make her feel better." He removed a piece of straw from King's mane. "They're likely to return without warning."

"They wouldn't do that."

"You're sure?" He looked dubious. "It's not every day their only child becomes the target of a criminal."

Cassie's throat tightened. Was he worried he'd be out of a job once her parents returned? Was he starting to dread leaving the ranch? Leaving her?

She already knew her heart would be bruised and sad if he left. *Not if, Cassie. He is going to leave eventually. He prefers the open road and limitless opportunities to putting down roots in one place. He told you that from the start.*

"Of course they'd rather be here. But they know I'm not alone."

He shoved his boot in the stirrup and hauled himself smoothly into the saddle. Although solidly built, he moved with grace and efficiency.

Cassie shook her head. She had to stop noticing these things.

They finished the first pasture and returned to the barn. After watering the horses, Luke went to get a sack off the shelf. One of the barn cats twisted between his boots, and Luke stumbled sideways as he tried to avoid stepping on him. He took the full weight of the feed sack onto his shoulder. Groaning, he dropped the sack to the ground and gripped it. Beads of sweat popped onto his forehead, and his face had a gray cast.

"You need to sit." Cassie put a hand on his lower back and tried not to notice the ripple of muscle beneath his shirt. She guided him over to a barrel and gently pushed him onto it. "Now, what's going on with that shoulder? You've favored it since I met you."

He grimaced. "I had surgery on it not so long ago."

She gasped. "And you've been doing manual labor? Were you cleared by a doctor?"

His silence was answer enough.

"You're not lifting another finger on my ranch until you see someone."

"I'll be as good as new tomorrow."

She retrieved his coat from the hook where he'd hung it. "Let's go. I'm taking you to the urgent care clinic."

He blinked at her. "Cassie—"

"No arguing, cowboy."

Scowling, he slowly got to his feet. "I didn't know you were hiding a bossy streak behind that sweet exterior."

She snorted. "I teach high school students for a living."

"Yeah, well, I'm not a teenager," he groused.

"Trust me, I know," she muttered, helping him ease into his coat.

He arched a brow at her, and a humorous twinkle entered his eyes. His face was very near, and she caught the ever so slight uptick of his mouth. Her face flamed. Still clutching his coat lapels, she got snared in his gaze and felt as if she were tipping into the dazzling depths.

His hands found her waist, the pressure so light she wasn't sure he was actually touching her. Blood rushed through her ears. Luke made her feel more alive than she'd ever felt before, and that was extremely dangerous.

"You're not staying in Tulip forever."

He visibly swallowed. "No, I'm not."

"And I'm not ready for another relationship." Although difficult to admit, it had to be said. "I thought I could trust Brian since I'd known him my whole life. Turns out he wasn't worthy of my heart."

His hands fell to his sides. His handsome features closed her out, becoming stoic and almost harsh. "I apologize for making you uncomfortable."

She reluctantly released his coat lapels, a cold shiver sweeping over her. At this moment, she was reminded that Luke Fisher was a mystery, despite the recent situations that had pushed them together. If she couldn't trust a man she'd known her whole life, how could she get involved with a man she'd known for a few weeks?

NINE

Luke hadn't liked his family or friends fussing over him during his recovery, so he was surprised to find he didn't mind Cassie's nurturing ways. As soon as they'd returned from the clinic, she'd ordered him onto the couch and draped a blanket over his lap. She'd brought him a snack and handed him the TV remote.

"What else can I get you?"

She stood between him and the entertainment center. Her French braid had lost its tidiness in the hours since breakfast, and tendrils formed a halo around her oval face. As she applied gloss to her lips, the faint scent of cinnamon wafted over. He closed his eyes. She had no idea the inner debate her very presence created. That moment in the barn earlier this morning had tested his integrity in a way it had never been tested. He'd yearned to feel her lips beneath his. He was lonely after all these weeks away from home, but that wasn't the reason he'd wanted to kiss Cassie West. He was starting to like her. *Really* like her.

Kissing her under any circumstances would be foolhardy. Kissing her while pretending to be someone else? Unacceptable.

"Are you in pain?"

The cushion beside him dipped. He opened his eyes. "The medicine I took at the clinic is kicking in."

"I'm not sure I like this wait and see approach. Maybe we should head on in to the Mayfield hospital."

He was tempted to rub away the wrinkle between her brows.

"The X-ray didn't show any new damage. I promise I'll get an MRI if my shoulder doesn't improve in a few days."

"Well, until then, you're to stay on this couch with Dusty."

At the sound of his name, Dusty trotted in from the kitchen and hopped up on Luke's other side. "I'm allowed to do light chores."

Standing, she crossed her arms. "Not today, you're not. We'll have to wait and see what tomorrow brings."

At the sound of an approaching vehicle, Cassie crossed to the windows and shifted aside the curtain. "What are Nash and Skye doing here, I wonder?"

"You weren't expecting them?"

She shook her head. "I texted them from the clinic. They have Eden with them, and Nash is carrying a stack of covered dishes. They must've brought a meal for you."

"For me?" Luke was astounded. "Why?"

"Because they like you and want to show their support?" Laughing, she opened the door and greeted the trio.

Luke pushed the blanket aside and got to his feet as Skye walked in carrying little Eden. She wiggled out of Skye's hold and rushed over to the couch to pet the friendly dog.

"Gentle," Skye reminded.

With her chin-length blond hair and curious blue eyes, Eden was unmistakably a Wilder. Luke was very aware that she was his one and only niece. Resuming his seat, he smiled at her.

"Hi, I'm Luke."

Eden smiled shyly. "My name is Eden Louise Wilder."

"That's a very pretty name."

"I'm sorry to hear you've been consigned to the couch,"

Skye said, remaining on the other side of the coffee table. "You're in good hands with Cassie, though."

After placing the casserole dishes on the island, Nash returned to Skye's side. "How long are you out of commission?"

"I could've done light chores today, but Cassie has forbidden me. Hopefully, I can get back to normal tomorrow." Luke gestured to the kitchen. "Thanks for the food. It was mighty kind of you."

Nash curved his arm around Skye's waist. "It was Skye's idea."

Cassie clapped her hands together. "Does that mean you brought some of your famous waffles?"

"Maple pecan. For tomorrow's breakfast."

She shielded one side of her mouth. "Or dessert," she mock whispered to Luke, winking.

He was happy to see her worries momentarily set aside. "I won't tell if you won't."

Looking at the couple, Luke intercepted Nash's inquisitive expression. Was he wondering if Luke was hiding any more secrets?

Cassie perched on the arm of the couch while Skye and Nash got cozy on the loveseat. Still enamored with the dog, Eden clambered up, squeezing in between Luke and Dusty.

Skye cocked her head to one side. "Luke, I don't know how I never noticed your eyes are the Wilder electric blue. Don't you agree, Nash?"

Luke could barely breathe as Nash's gaze narrowed. He felt Cassie's gaze on him, too.

"You're not a long-lost Wilder cousin, are you?" Cassie teased.

His mouth felt like it was stuffed with marbles. He was tempted to confess everything right then and there. The memory of the day he'd learned the truth about his biological father kept him quiet.

Wes Wilder had rejected him before he'd even been born. He hadn't even wanted to meet him. The emotional toll had been devastating. It had taken years for Luke to work through the layers of anger, hurt and bitterness. Putting himself on the line now, when he was grieving his partner and wrestling with survivor's guilt, was too much.

Nash shrugged. "We're not the only ones with that particular shade of blue."

"Those eyes are the reason I believed Lucy's claim that you were Eden's father," Skye reminded.

"And her blond hair," he responded, tweaking one of Skye's curls. "Luke's hair is the same color as yours."

She playfully batted his hand away, and the subject was dropped. Luke's breathing gradually evened out.

"What's going on at the school today?" Skye asked.

"The insurance adjuster is supposed to get the ball rolling on replacing the cafeteria window. We'll have to install plywood boards until the new glass can be ordered. There wasn't any other damage. The crime scene techs should be finished today as well." She turned to Luke. "That reminds me, Thomas had to leave the farm after lunch. I told him I'd resume the care of the animals this evening. I'll have to go in around six."

"I'll go with you."

"As long as you promise not to lift a finger."

He might not be at the top of his game physically, but he would be armed with his service weapon. He could still protect her.

Her phone beeped. Leaning forward, she grabbed it off the coffee table and read the screen. "It's an email from Gabriela. We're having classes tomorrow. The Winter Wonderland dance is going on as scheduled. I completely forgot about it."

Nash frowned. "Aren't those usually held in the gym?"

She kept skimming. "Bob and Kelly Winfield have offered the use of their barn venue facilities as long as we have hired security."

"That's thoughtful of them." Skye held up her hand. "I'll volunteer for security duty."

Nash nodded. "Count me in."

"Don't forget me," Luke added.

"Cassie's a chaperone and will need someone with her," Skye said. "You should go as her date."

Cassie's cheeks pinked, and she rolled her eyes. "Ignore her."

"It's a good idea. I don't have anything suitable to wear, though."

"You and Nash are about the same height and size." Skye looked at her fiancé. "I'm sure he has something you can borrow."

Nash shrugged. "Feel free to shop in my closet."

Luke's throat constricted. He didn't realize until this moment how much he longed to be accepted by his siblings and to establish a connection with them. If he did come clean, would they be able to look past the subterfuge?

"You shouldn't have encouraged Luke to be my date."

This was Cassie's first chance to take Skye to task. Her friend was stationed outside the entrance of the rustic barn-turned-event space. Teenagers streamed past in their festive dresses and dapper suits. Music leaked outside. Gauging from the beat, this was no slow-dance situation. The butterflies that had been accumulating all day made themselves known. Did Luke prefer to dance the night away or sip punch on the sidelines? Even though the night air had a wintry bite, her palms felt damp. She checked her upswept hair again, testing the pins.

"Stop fussing," Skye ordered. "Your hair and makeup are flawless. I'm thrilled you chose the red dress. Did Luke's eyes pop out of his head?"

The memory of how his eyes had widened and his lips had parted when she emerged from the bedroom sent warmth washing over her. "Stop. He's my employee."

Cassie turned to observe Luke and Nash, who were standing between the corner of the barn and an old Hummer. He looked dashing in the borrowed black suit. A white shirt and black-and-white-striped tie completed the elegant look. His raven hair, brushed off his forehead and held with styling product, glinted in the moonlight.

"There's more between you than work," she insisted. "I've sensed a vibe between you. Nash has, too."

Cassie tugged her coat sleeves down and curled her fingers inside. "I don't know hardly anything about him. Look what happened with Brian."

"Exactly. You grew up with Brian and thought you knew everything there was to know about him. You thought there wouldn't be any surprises."

She'd certainly never dreamed he would drop her three months before their wedding. "I can't think about romance right now anyway."

"Love sometimes grows in the most surprising of times."

Skye spoke from experience. She and Nash might not have ended up together if she hadn't been appointed his bodyguard. Trouble had thrown them together and something beautiful had resulted. Cassie didn't hold the same hope for herself.

Luke joined them, and after a brief word to Skye, he accompanied Cassie inside. Twinkly blue and white lights were draped from the ceiling in a crisscross pattern, illuminating the cozy space. Blue, white and silver balloon arches created various photo-op stations around the room. Glass dispensers with lemonade and punch were stationed on the tables to their right, along with platters of cookies and brownies. The dance area spread from the far end where the DJ was stationed to just inside the door. A section of tables and chairs offered a chance to relax and enjoy a snack. Fortunately, the music volume didn't prohibit normal conversation.

Luke scanned the room as if familiarizing himself with the layout and exit points. She'd seen Remi and Skye do the same thing. It wasn't the first time she'd had the impression that perhaps he'd had a different career prior to being a ranch hand. Before she could formulate a question, he turned to her.

"There are a lot of adults here tonight. Is that typical?"

She looked around, noticing the parents grouped around the room, many appearing to be in deep conversation. "No, it's not. Some of the teachers thought the dance should've been canceled in light of what happened Monday night. I assume many of the parents feel the same."

When classes resumed on Wednesday, students and teachers had been on edge despite the presence of law enforcement. The plywood in the cafeteria was a reminder of the terrifying breach in their school. Most teachers and staff had been openly sympathetic to her ordeal. Did the few who hadn't reached out blame her?

Cassie unfastened the buttons on her coat and removed it, then hung it on a wall-mounted coatrack. When she rejoined Luke, he looked bemused.

"This brings back memories."

"You went to a lot of dances?"

"Almost all of them." He smiled. "I was on the football

team, so it was sort of expected. Those of us without dates went as a group."

"Football? You? I can't picture it."

He smirked. "I was quarterback."

"Ah. You must've been surrounded with admirers."

He shrugged in his nonchalant, humble manner. "I was blessed with good friends and didn't date seriously while in high school."

"That was mature of you. Have you ever been in a serious relationship?"

"The most serious one lasted eighteen months. She got a job offer in another state and didn't hesitate to end things between us."

"Ouch." Cassie sensed it wouldn't be easy to walk away from Luke. "Moving around from place to place must make it difficult to form connections."

Brow furrowing, he ran a finger under his collar. The upbeat song ended. The mood on the dance floor mellowed as a slow, dreamy love song came on. He held out his hand, palm up.

"Care to dance?"

She stared into his impossibly beautiful blue eyes and found herself debating the wisdom of accepting.

"Are chaperones allowed to dance?" he said, brows inching up.

"Yes, of course." She blew out a breath and took his hand.

He circumvented the thickest cluster of dancers and chose a spot between the DJ and one of the photo-op stations. He eased her closer and draped his arm around her, his hand splayed against the middle of her back. His fingertips seemed to brand her through the gauzy fabric of her gown. Lightheaded with anticipation, she slid her arms around his neck and locked her fingers where his hair met his suit collar. They swayed to the rhythm, making little half steps in a lazy circle, not talking as the crooning words wrapped around them.

Everyone else melted away. Luke was strong, handsome, kind and brave. He was a Christ-follower, a cowboy and a gentleman… Her dream guy.

Did it matter that she didn't know what kind of music he liked or if he was grumpy when he was sick? He didn't know every little detail about her, either.

Could she finally move past the shock and humiliation of Brian's rejection? Should she take a chance on Luke despite the inherent risks?

She delved her fingertips into his soft hair. His gaze became hooded, and his hand slowly slid up her back to cup her neck. Goose bumps danced across her skin. She was positive he would've kissed her if they were alone.

"Excuse me, can I cut in?"

Jim Hallman's voice sliced through her contentment. Luke's expression shuttered, and he reluctantly released her and walked away. Jim instantly took his place. Swallowing her disappointment, she pasted on a smile as he grasped her left hand and rested his other on her waist.

"How did you get roped into chaperoning?" she asked. "Don't you normally avoid these things?"

His eyes were grave, his mouth unsmiling. "I wanted to be here for you, Cassie."

"That's thoughtful of you, Jim, but we have plenty of security." In addition to Nash and Skye, Sheriff Hines and his deputies were on hand to ward off trouble.

"I have to be sure you're safe."

His tone and the way he looked at her unnerved her. To her dismay, the song transitioned to another slow number.

"I am safe," she insisted. "Luke's with me. You don't have to stick around. Why don't you go home to Tracy? How has she been, anyway? I haven't seen her in a while."

"Tracy is fine." His eyes flickered. "Cassie, I don't like how much time you're spending with Fisher. You're too good for that no-account drifter."

She stiffened. "Please don't say that."

He continued as if she hadn't spoken. "That termite Brian treated you with disrespect. He was a fool to leave you." His fingers tightened on her waist. "I'm worried you're headed for another broken heart. Please heed my warning and steer clear of Fisher."

"I'm uncomfortable with this conversation." She slipped her hand free and stepped back, forcing him to drop his arm.

"Wait." He snagged her wrist. "I didn't mean to anger you."

Although she'd worked alongside Jim Hallman for several years, she was seeing a new side of him. A scary side.

Luke didn't trust Jim. Could Jim's unusual interest in her signal a deeper, more disturbing truth? Could he be the one behind the attacks?

TEN

Luke gulped down the tart lemonade. No more dancing, McCoy.

He'd known it was a bad idea, but he'd had to do something to distract her from asking questions he wasn't prepared to answer. He couldn't see her and Hallman from the refreshment table. Probably a good thing. His respiratory system needed a break.

As soon as she'd exited the bedroom, he'd known he was in trouble. Her transition from casual cowgirl to elegant lady had almost knocked him flat. Her blond hair had been coiled into a sophisticated twist. Tiny silver earrings glistened in her ears. Her makeup was soft and inviting, her skin fresh and shimmery. The shoulders and sleeves of her red dress were a sheer, gauzy material, and the solid panels nipped in at the waist before flaring to mid-calf. He'd wished there were no secrets between them, no barriers and no reasons why he couldn't date her for real.

He tossed the cup in the garbage. This wasn't a date. He was her self-appointed bodyguard.

The dancers parted, and he glimpsed Cassie's unhappy expression. He charged through the middle of the dance floor. Cassie shook off Hallman's hand. The gym teacher noticed Luke. Scowling, he spun and stalked in the direction of the bathrooms.

Luke met up with her near the coatrack. "Cassie."

She pivoted. "I just had an unusual exchange with Jim. He wasn't acting like a married man, I can tell you that."

"What did he say?"

Cassie relayed the conversation, which led Luke to wonder if Jim had an unhealthy obsession.

"When was Tracy Hallman last seen?"

"I have no idea." Her brow furrowed. "Do you think he'd hurt her?"

"That depends. If he's created a fantasy in his head about you, he might see her as an obstacle to be removed."

"Let's assume our theory is right. Why would he attack me if he imagines himself in love with me?"

"If he thinks he can't have you or if he doesn't approve of how you're acting, he could become full of rage and lash out." He searched for Jim in the crowd. "We should ask Sheriff Hines to do a welfare check on Tracy."

"I hope I'm not reading too much into this." Cassie bit her lower lip. "Jim's a somber guy and a loner, but he's a good teacher and coach. The students respond to him. I've never gotten wind of complaints."

"If he's innocent of wrongdoing, then he has nothing to worry about."

Luke continued to scan the room. Where had Jim disappeared to? His gaze landed on Morgan Tucker. Slipping behind a panel of floor-length streamers, she glanced around as if to make sure no one was watching before darting out a side exit.

"Where do you think Morgan is going?"

Cassie's gaze followed his. "I'm not sure. Her friends are still dancing."

"Did she come with a date?"

"No. Evan, her dad, has a no dating until after graduation rule."

"Is he here tonight?"

"He and Arianna bought tickets to a musical playing in Mayfield."

"When the cat's away…"

She gave a matter-of-fact nod. "We should follow her."

They exited through the same door Morgan had used. This side of the barn wasn't meant for visitor use. A gravel drive wound to a smaller barn and outbuildings beneath the trees. Across from the door, a barbed wire fence enclosed fields likely used for grazing. A car's taillights glowed in the darkness. A motion light flickered on, illuminating Morgan locked in the arms of a stranger.

Cassie tugged on his hand, and he went with her to investigate. The sound of their approach alerted the couple, and they broke apart. The man obviously wasn't a high school student. Around six feet with an athletic build, he looked much older than Morgan.

"Miss West! What are you doing out here?"

"The better question is, what are you doing out here?"

Morgan glanced at her feet. The man murmured something in her ear before getting into the car and driving away. That raised a red flag in Luke's mind.

"Who is that, Morgan?" Cassie's tone was mild, but her face was wreathed in concern.

She lifted her head and jutted her chin. "I'm eighteen. I can date who I want."

"Have you had that discussion with your dad?"

Her jaw tightened as she flipped her long hair behind her shoulder. "I'll be out of the house in a few months. He won't have any control over what I do."

"He loves you, Morgan. He wants the best for you."

Luke spoke up. "Is your boyfriend's age the reason you're hiding out here in the shadows?"

Her eyes flared. "Twelve years is nothing."

Cassie gasped. "He's thirty?"

Morgan's show of defiance gave way to pleading. "He's everything I've ever dreamed of, Miss West. He's sweet and kind and smart. Please don't say anything to my dad or Arianna."

"I didn't recognize him," Cassie said. "Where does he live? Did you meet him online?"

"I'm not that naïve. I know what can happen. Thomas and he are friends. They have classes together at the community college. He's also a manager at a bookstore in Mayfield. He came to the barn with Thomas a couple of months ago, and we struck up a conversation. He's very easy to talk to."

"Morgan, you have to tell your father."

"What? No! He'll make me stop seeing him."

"You'll be graduating in May," Luke reminded her. "If he's serious about you, he'll wait."

A flashlight strobed over them. "Everything all right out here?" Deputy Flowers called out.

"We're fine," Luke responded.

Nodding, the deputy walked back the way he came. Morgan dashed past them.

"Morgan, wait," Cassie called, sighing when the teen didn't respond. "I didn't see this coming. Morgan's been a stellar student from the time she joined the ag program and has been really focused on academic excellence. I did notice she's been distracted in recent weeks, and she's forgotten to turn in a couple of assignments. I chalked it up to senioritis. Seniors get antsy, especially in the spring semester."

"What are you going to do?"

Shivering, she chafed her arms. "As her teacher, I feel like I have to do something. I'll speak to her again on Monday. If she doesn't agree to come clean, I'll have to have an unpleasant conversation with Evan."

He glanced around, not liking that they were alone in the dark. "It's cold. Let's go back inside."

Once back inside the venue, Luke was determined not to ask her for any more dances. He remained on the sidelines whenever she was invited to dance. Of course, she was a popular partner. His insides wound tighter as the night went on, although most of the men were fathers of her students and happily married. The science teacher, Fallon Roberts, danced with her three times. He was divorced and single, according to Cassie. Luke couldn't tell if the man was interested in Cassie or merely comfortable in her presence.

Not that it mattered. Someday soon, Luke would be leaving Cassie behind. Even if he came clean to his siblings, and they agreed to build a relationship, he didn't plan on staying in Tulip.

Cassie would continue working the ranch and teaching her students. She'd live her life and eventually find love, get married and have children.

On the dance floor, Fallon whirled her around and dipped her, and she laughed out loud. Luke ground his teeth together. The evening couldn't end soon enough.

A bit later, after saying goodbye to Skye and Nash, they headed back to the ranch.

"I'll take a look through the house before checking on the animals," he told her, locking up the truck.

"I'll help you as soon as I change."

They'd left the porch lights on, as well as lamps in the living room. He quickly made the rounds and didn't see anything out of place. Cassie let Dusty inside, and he greeted them with enthusiasm.

Luke put his hand in his suit pocket to retrieve his phone. Dusty jumped up, eager for Luke's ear rubs. He removed his hand quickly to keep the dog from dirtying Nash's suit, inadvertently dislodging his wallet. The wallet hit the floor near Cassie's feet and flopped open.

The kitchen light glinted on his police badge.

Luke's muscles locked up as Cassie bent to retrieve it. Her nose crinkled as she studied his driver's license.

Her brown eyes filled with confusion. "Why does this say your name is Luke McCoy?"

The guilt stamped on Luke's face amplified Cassie's distress. She studied the license again. He'd said he was from Texas, and the address confirmed that. She tilted the badge so that the lamp light caught the words. Detective. San Antonio PD.

"Are you a cop?"

He stood statue-still, his blue eyes watchful. "Yes."

All the signs had been there. The way he'd gone after her attacker. His air of authority around other law enforcement. His habit of facing the entrance in public establishments and his keen awareness of his surroundings.

"Are you here undercover for a case? Is that why you used a fake surname and hid your real profession?"

Wincing, he shook his head. "I'm not here on assignment. I came to Tulip for personal reasons."

He hadn't come on official police business. His decision to cover up his real identity didn't have anything to do with seeking justice or capturing a criminal. What other purpose could there be that was honorable?

"Promise me you'll hear me out."

"I'm not promising you anything." She paced the length of the entertainment center. "You insinuated yourself into my home and my life, and I don't even know who you are!"

How naïve she'd been. Fooled by kind manners and a lazy smile. She should've done her research. Should've heeded Remi's advice.

"It's true you don't know some specifics about me, but

I wasn't pretending to be a different person. I'm the same man you danced with earlier."

She flung out her arms. "I danced with a fraud."

His brows drew together. "Please let me explain."

"How do I know you won't feed me more lies?"

"You know my real name and address. You can do an internet search."

Stopping short, she folded her arms across her chest and glared at him. "Something I should've done before I let you step foot on my ranch."

He removed his suit jacket, loosened his tie and thrust his hands in his pant pockets. "I grew up believing Ian McCoy was my father. Shortly after high school graduation, I was sifting through papers in my mom's desk and discovered a letter from Wes Wilder. It was clearly a response to my mother, acknowledging that I was his child."

Cassie gasped and clapped her hand over her mouth.

"I confronted my mom. She explained that prior to her marriage to Ian, she met a rancher from Mississippi. He was in town to purchase cattle and invited her to dinner. He returned to town once a month for the next year, and they had a fling. She fancied herself in love. When she learned she was pregnant, she decided to deliver the news in person. She was stunned to discover Wes was married with a young son. He told her in no uncertain terms that he wanted nothing to do with her or their baby. He already had a family. He warned her not to make trouble. Heartbroken, she returned to San Antonio to raise me alone. She met Ian when I was nine months old. They got married and later had my sister, Paige. They decided that concealing the truth would spare me pain."

Cassie lowered her hand to her side, stunned that she was looking at Nash and Remi's half brother. "You have the Wilder eyes."

"Everything else I got from my mom's side."

Cassie thought he had the same chin and mouth as Nash, but their very different coloring had kept her from making the connection.

"Why wait until now to come here? You could've come when you first learned the truth. Wes was still alive then."

"The discovery put me into an emotional tailspin. I began to question everything I thought I knew to be true about myself and my life. I was angry with my mom and Ian. I was angry at this callous stranger who'd treated my mom like dirt and who didn't want to meet me, his own flesh and blood. I figured if he didn't want me in his life before, why would he change his mind?"

"So why now?" she repeated. "After all these years?"

He paused a beat—a sign he was holding something back?

"I was home on medical leave and had time on my hands, so I decided to learn more about my siblings."

Suspicion swirled. "You're on leave because of your shoulder?"

Shadows filtered across his face. "Yes."

"During your research, you surely found out how much the Wilder enterprise is worth. Are you unable to return to your job? Is that the real reason you came here? You thought you'd get to know them and figure out a way to get your hands on some of the money?"

"No." His face reddened. "My position is waiting on me when I'm physically fit to return. I don't need or want their money."

"Then explain the need for secrecy."

"I wanted to get to know them without the suspicions and questions. I wanted to decide on my terms whether to risk getting rejected again."

Cassie mulled over this admission. He looked sincere. While she could understand his fear of rejection, she couldn't move past the secrecy. Her throat thickened with unshed tears. "You're a detective. Digging into people's lives is your job. You wouldn't have stopped with their careers or habits or places they frequent. No, you would've learned about the important people in their lives. You came to Tulip knowing about me, Remi's closest friend. You couldn't have known about my need of a ranch hand, though."

She recalled that day in the café when she'd come in for recommendations. Luke had overheard her conversation with the customers and offered his services. He'd been in town a few days and had already made a positive impression on the owner, the waitresses and the old coots who used the Pit Stop as their social club. She'd thought he was an unasked-for blessing.

"This job gave me a reason to stick around," he said carefully.

"You used me." Her stomach burned. "You used me to get close to Nash and Remi. You pumped me for information. I was your unwitting informant."

"I'm sorry."

"Your apology is nothing but empty words." Cassie swallowed past the lump in her throat. "I want you gone by dawn."

ELEVEN

Luke spent an uncomfortable night in his truck. Unwilling to leave her unprotected, he'd parked outside her front door without her knowledge. Long before sunrise the next morning, he packed his meager belongings and cleaned the loft apartment. After that was done, he postponed his departure by knocking out a few chores for Cassie. He thought of everything that needed attention on the ranch and wondered who was going to do it. There were only so many hours in a day. Cassie couldn't do everything. She couldn't be alone here considering there was a target on her back.

He finished mucking the stalls and glanced around at the barn that had been his home for more than a month.

Face it, McCoy. There aren't enough chores in the world to make up for the hurt you've caused her.

Stalking to the door, he leaned against the jamb. The sun was peeking over the horizon, spraying yellow-pink light over the fields. The chickens were stirring in their henhouse, and a pair of ducks waddled through the yard. He'd never forget his time on the West ranch.

He'd never forget the owner, either. Had Cassie gotten any sleep? Had she called Remi and told her everything? Strange, now that the truth was out, he was more concerned about Cassie's reaction than his siblings'. She'd accused him of using her, as if she meant nothing to him. That simply wasn't the case. He'd quickly come to like and admire her.

His chest grew tight remembering the hurt in her pretty doe eyes. Now that she'd had time to mull over his revelation, would she be more receptive to his apology?

Cameron Hersh's image popped up on his phone screen. Retreating into the barn, he accepted the video call.

"What's so urgent you're calling this early?" Luke greeted. "Is Amber okay?"

Cameron sat at his office desk, the harsh fluorescent lights revealing his bloodshot eyes and mussed hair. "She's fine. I couldn't sleep thanks to you."

"Me? What did I do?"

"You sent me on a hunt, that's what, and I've discovered that your theory has merit."

Luke's stomach tightened into a ball. "What did you find out?"

"I started with the towns closest to Tulip and Mayfield. I didn't find any victims matching Miss West or Miss Moody's descriptions. However, when I widened the search to a two-hundred-mile radius, I found eleven women who've died under mysterious circumstances. Their cases were never solved." He paused, his frown deepening. "Every single one is close in age to Cassie, and each one looks enough like her to be related."

He sank onto a barrel and thrust his hand through his hair. "Eleven."

Eleven lives—twelve counting Hana Moody—cut short at the hand of a predator, possibly the same man who'd come after Cassie. What could be his motive?

"There could be more. I haven't yet expanded the search."

"Have you uncovered any connections between the victims?"

Shaking his head, he tipped a chipped mug to his mouth. "I've been buried in cases. I came in early to work on this."

"I appreciate it. Send me the information you've gathered so far, and I'll take it to Detective Kane. He can take over from here."

"Listen, McCoy, a friendly word of advice." He glanced around the office and then lowered his voice. "I've heard rumblings that the chief is getting impatient with your prolonged absence. When are you coming home?"

The news that Luke's position at the department was in jeopardy wasn't welcome. It wasn't surprising, either. He'd been gone a long time. Although he dreaded the thought of returning to work and facing Simon's glaring absence, he'd assumed he would go back eventually. Police work was his life.

But the possibility that Cassie had become a target of a serial killer meant he couldn't leave her unprotected. He had to convince her to let him stay.

Cassie yanked open the door. "You could've left the key inside the apartment."

Her voice was harsh and almost unrecognizable to her ears. Jutting her chin, she hardened her heart against Luke's obvious distress. His eyes were bloodshot, and his raven waves unruly. A shadow of a beard darkened his cheeks, lending him a rakish air. Bits of hay clung to his brown and blue flannel shirt.

Images of the news articles she'd pored over last night surged into her sleep-deprived mind. Luke being hoisted on a stretcher with a burned-out garage in the background. Luke in his official police portrait, handsome and oh so serious in his uniform.

As soon as he'd retreated to his quarters in the barn, she'd taken out her laptop and started searching, hungry for information about the man she'd employed and befriended. *And trusted*, she added.

Although Brian had broken her trust, he hadn't callously used her for his own ends.

"I have news about your case," he stated. "May I come in?"

Cassie retreated to the kitchen island without answering him.

He closed the door behind him, crossed to the island and sank his hands in his pockets. "I asked a colleague of mine at the SAPD to look into the possibility of a serial killer at work. He found eleven women who match your description and who were strangled with a thin leather belt—all within two hundred miles of Tulip."

Her knees went weak. She dropped her phone onto the counter. This hadn't started with her, as she'd thought. "What brought him here to my school?"

"I don't have any answers. Hersh is sending me the information, which I plan to take to Kane."

She nodded numbly, fear settling like a cold fog inside her. A man who enjoyed killing women had decided he wanted her dead because she had blond hair and brown eyes and fit a certain weight and height category.

"Cassie, I'd like your permission to stay."

"Stay?"

He started to round the island to her side. Cassie bolted upright, and he stopped at the corner.

"I'm trained to protect people," he said quietly. "You're in danger. If our theory is correct, and we are dealing with a serial killer, he won't quit until he's accomplished his goal. He's very skilled at evading the police."

Dread of facing her would-be killer again shuddered through her. How would she manage to get a wink of sleep with just her and Dusty on the ranch? How would the animals fare with her work responsibilities tearing her away?

"Why do you want to stay? Why put your life on the line for me? I'm merely a means to an end," she bit out.

"That may have been true in the beginning. It's not now. I think you're a wonderful person, Cassie," he said earnestly. "I've seen your tireless commitment to your students and to this community. When I leave Tulip, I want to leave confident you're going to be safe."

Her heart yearned to believe him. Despite his underhanded behavior, she still liked this man. Did that make her a fool?

"I came to Tulip carrying a whole lot of baggage," he continued. "Truth is, I was running from my own guilt. I lost my partner, Simon, in a fire. I had too much time on my hands, time to dwell on the reason I wasn't at work. That's why I decided to finally travel to Mississippi and meet my siblings. Working on your ranch was a chance for me to clear my head. I was too busy and exhausted to think about my mistakes."

Sadness carved lines about his mouth, and his eyes were haunted.

"I read about the fire and your partner's death."

He swallowed hard. "Simon and I were closing in on a powerful drug runner, and his crew got the jump on us. Locked us in that garage and set it on fire. We did everything we could to escape, but…" Compressing his lips, he shook his head and stared out the window.

Cassie clenched her fists. His anguish was palpable, and she longed to comfort him. The horror of what she'd read didn't begin to measure up to what he'd experienced that day. He obviously blamed himself for failing to save his partner.

She debated what to do. He was offering to stay on. Why not let him? She still needed a ranch hand, and he was a skilled bodyguard. Yes, he'd hurt her. He'd made her feel stupid for believing the best of people. She'd just gotten her confidence back and had even felt hopeful that romance was possible. In one moment, he'd shattered all that.

It wasn't like she'd fallen in love with him, though. She could guard her heart. She'd been doing it ever since Brian walked away from her and the future they'd planned.

"If I had another option, I wouldn't agree to your offer," she said. "I don't."

He stood taller. "You can trust me to keep you safe, Cassie."

That was the only thing she trusted him with—her physical safety.

"There's one thing you have to do first."

"Anything."

"You have to tell Remi and Nash the truth."

His chest expanded, and he slowly nodded.

"Today," she added.

"Okay."

Cassie fired off a group text to Nash and Remi, indicating she needed to see them about an urgent matter. They responded almost simultaneously. Remi wasn't scheduled to work, so she was spending the day assisting Nash on the ranch.

Within the hour, Luke was driving them to the Wilder ranch. This time, the silence between them wasn't companionable or comfortable. Cassie snuck frequent glances at his shuttered expression and questioned whether compelling him to have this confrontation was the right thing to do. But she refused to cover for him.

When they arrived, Nash waved them into the workshop and the newly rebuilt calf barn attached to it.

"What's on your mind?" Nash said, wiping the grease off his hands. Tools were spread out beside an ATV.

Remi stepped through the door connecting the two

buildings cradling an orange-and-white kitten in her arms. She wore an Ole Miss sweatshirt and jeans, her straight blond hair tucked into a ponytail and threaded through her ball cap. "Morning, guys." Her eyes were curious. "There's a fresh pot of coffee and a box of donuts on the counter over there if you're interested."

Cassie declined, as did Luke. When neither spoke, Nash arched a blond brow and planted his hands on his hips. "Is this about the case?"

Cassie glanced at Luke. He looked as if he might lose his breakfast.

"There has been a development," she said, "but we can talk about that later."

Remi put the kitten on a ragged dog bed in the corner and came to stand beside Nash. "Must be serious. Luke, you okay? You look feverish."

He removed his Stetson and gripped it in both hands.

"This isn't easy for me to say," he began, clearing his throat.

Moved by his plight, Cassie shifted closer and put her hand on his arm. His blue eyes cut to hers, shimmery with gratitude. She nodded in encouragement.

"My last name isn't Fisher. It's McCoy. I'm a detective with the San Antonio Police Department. The reason I'm in Tulip is because my biological father is from here." He paused, crumpling the brim of his hat in his grip.

Remi's brow creased. "Who?"

"Wes Wilder."

TWELVE

Luke thought his heart was going to explode.

Remi's jaw sagged. Nash's blond brows crashed down.

"This is a prank, right?" he demanded. "Some kind of crass joke?"

"What's going on, Cassie?" Remi demanded, anger seeping into her eyes. Twin spots of color bit her cheeks.

Cassie removed her hand from his arm, but she remained beside him. The woman amazed him. She was a true diamond among pearls. In the midst of her hurt, she offered him support. Comfort.

"Cassie learned my true identity last night," Luke said, "She's the reason I'm here now."

Nash crossed his arms over his chest. "Our father was a lot of things, but he wasn't a cheater."

"He loved our mother," Remi contended. "I don't know what sort of lies you've been fed, but you're not a Wilder."

"Maybe he made up the lies." Nash's eyes narrowed. "What exactly are you after?"

Cassie stepped to the side, her hand lifted as if to pause the brewing storm. "He has the Wilder eyes."

Remi shook her head. "That doesn't prove his claim."

"Look closer," Cassie urged. "Don't you think he and Nash have the same shaped mouth? A similar jawline?"

Remi reluctantly compared Luke's features to Nash's. "It's easy to see whatever we want to see."

"My mother has a letter from Wes confirming I was the product of their affair."

"Where is this letter? I want to see it," Remi said.

"I left in a hurry and didn't think to bring proof."

"Who is your mother?" Nash said. "Did she live around here?"

"Her name is Deborah. She's lived her whole life on the outskirts of San Antonio. Wes traveled there many times to buy cattle. According to my mom, they hit it off. She didn't know he was married and thought they had a future together."

Nash looked away, the muscle in his jaw twitching. Remi's face got redder.

"I have a photo of them together." Luke removed the worn, faded photo from his wallet and handed it over.

The pair inspected the couple in the photo. Remi's mouth tightened. "This doesn't prove your story."

Nash rubbed his jaw and turned to Remi. "Dad traveled to Texas multiple times a year before and after I was born."

"You believe him?" she demanded, flinging out her hand. "Look at how he deceived Cassie and the entire town, insinuating he was a drifter who just happened to roll in on the breeze."

Cassie clasped her hands tightly before her, her gaze downcast. He gritted his teeth.

Nash pinned Luke with his gaze. "You're willing to submit to a DNA test, I presume?"

"Of course."

"If the results confirm your claim, we'll sit down and discuss the next steps. We'll both need to hire lawyers."

Luke held up his hand. "Hold up a second. I don't want anything from you. If my mom or I cared about material gain, we could've come after Wes years ago. When she found out she was pregnant, she came looking for him, thinking he'd be thrilled. He informed her that he was married and that he already had a young son. He didn't need another. Mom returned to Texas and raised me with the support of my grandparents. Then she met Ian, my stepdad, and they decided it was kinder to let me believe my biological father was dead."

Nash's frown deepened. Remi's flush of anger faded, leaving her pale and wary. He didn't blame them for their reaction. He'd feel the same if the situation were reversed.

"I was eighteen when I learned the truth, and I was as angry as you are now. I eventually accepted that they'd done it to protect me. After all, what child wouldn't be devastated to know his parent didn't think he was worthy to meet, much less get to know or love?" Those old feelings of inadequacy and hurt clawed to the surface.

"I decided I didn't need to risk another rejection. I had two loving parents and a younger sister, Paige, who I adore. Grandparents. Aunts and uncles. Cousins. I tried to bury that part of me that yearned to know about Wes and any other family I had."

"What changed?" Nash asked.

His mouth was dry. "I almost died a few months ago. It made me think about the part of my heritage I hadn't explored, and I had regrets."

The ensuing silence threatened to choke him.

"I don't know what to believe," Remi said unhappily.

Luke screwed up his courage. "I'd like to get to know you both and to learn about my father and extended family. Take all the time you need." He turned to Cassie. "Are you going home with me? I can come back later and pick you up if you want to stick around a while longer."

Her blond brows tucked together. "I'd like to stay."

"I'll take you home," Remi volunteered, looking less sure of herself than usual.

Luke wished there could've been an easier way to deliver the news that had upended their world. As he returned to the West ranch alone, he asked for forgiveness and finally felt the weight of his secrets and lies lift. He'd been selfish, thinking only of his feelings and not Cassie's or his siblings'. He prayed for Nash and Remi, that they'd be able to work through their anger and disbelief and come to a place of acceptance. Finally, he prayed that he'd be granted a chance to be in their lives.

After pulling in to the ranch, he pulled out his phone and called his mom. The sight of her smiling face sent a bolt of homesickness through him.

"Luke, I'm so happy you called. Your dad and I just got back from the market." She bustled about the kitchen.

"I miss you," he blurted. "How's Paige?"

Her expression clouded, and she retreated into the sunroom. "What's happened, son?"

He shifted in the truck seat. "The cat's out of the bag. I'm afraid they didn't take it very well."

She inhaled sharply. "The Wilders have inflicted enough hurt on our family. Come home, Luke."

He thought about how crushed she must've been, a young woman pregnant and alone, rejected by the father of her unborn child. Wes had treated her with callous disdain, and there was nothing Luke could do to avenge her.

"The news is fresh. I'll give them time to absorb it." He paused. "There's another reason I can't come home yet."

"Oh?"

Luke told her about the attempts on Cassie's life.

"Please be careful," she said, not questioning his decision to protect his boss. "Cassie sounds like a wonderful young lady."

"She is, Mom."

There were many unresolved matters. Would Cassie forgive him? Would she ever trust him again? And what about Nash and Remi? Would they accept him into their lives?

All of it would have to be shelved until Cassie's attacker was captured. Her safety had to be his priority.

Cassie couldn't believe she was torn between comforting Luke and supporting her best friend. He'd looked surprisingly sad, as if he fully expected them to cut him out of their lives just as their father had. He'd left the photo of his mom and Wes with the siblings, and she studied it again. While Luke did have his mother's coloring, there were notable resemblances to Wes.

Seated at Nash's kitchen table, Remi huffed and shoved the laptop aside. "Leave it to a cop to have a bare bones social media presence."

She'd been researching Luke for the better part of an hour, just as Cassie had done the night before. "Did you read about the fire?"

Her lips compressed, and she tucked a wayward strand behind her ear. "Talk about irony. He and I are both detectives, and we've both spent the bulk of our careers going after drug pushers."

Cassie placed the photo on the table, and Remi picked it up. "You believe him, don't you?"

"I do." Cassie sighed. "I feel like I owe you an apology. If I had done what I should've done when hiring a new employee, I would've spared us all a lot of grief."

Remi dropped the photo and clasped Cassie's hand. "You have nothing to apologize for. This is all on him."

"Do *you* believe him?"

She sank back in her chair. "My father wasn't a model parent. However, I believe he truly loved my mom. It's difficult to imagine him being unfaithful to her." Her fingers tapped out an impatient rhythm on the wood. "On the other hand, he was a proud man and aware of his standing in the community. If Luke's claim is true, Dad wouldn't have wanted his reputation tarnished by a scandal of that magnitude."

The utility room door opened and closed, and Nash and his most trusted ranch hand, Hardy, entered the house.

"Skye's on her way home," Nash stated, looking as if the weight of the world was on his shoulders. He hadn't looked this grim since he and Skye had been under attack from an unknown enemy.

"I guess Eden wasn't happy about leaving the birthday party early." Remi sighed.

"Skye left her there. The other parents will keep an eye on her." He gestured to Hardy. The smoky-eyed, grizzled ranch hand had been in the Wilders' employ since Nash and Remi were teens. He was more like family than an employee, and he was as loyal to them as if they were his own kids. "I told Hardy everything. Thought he might have some insight on the situation."

Nash looked at Hardy, who grimly nodded. "Your father often traveled out of town in those days. I offered to go with him, but he said he liked the open road and the quiet. He and your mom were new parents, and they had different opinions on how things should be done. I reckon being sleep-deprived didn't help none. Wes made a few decisions that didn't pan out and cost him quite a sum of money. They were both under a lot of stress." He stopped and rubbed his jaw.

"Don't hold anything back on our account," Remi prompted.

"Wes never did tell me what he did or who he saw on those road trips, but I sensed something wasn't right. His trips became more frequent, and his reasons for going got real flimsy. Of course, I didn't question him. Then, not long after Nash's first birthday, the trips suddenly stopped."

Cassie watched the implications sink in on her friends' faces. Skye's truck rumbled into the drive, and Nash went outside to talk to her. Hardy also made a quick exit.

"Want me to whip up my mom's famous turtle pecan brownies?" Cassie asked. "They always did make you feel better."

Remi tossed the pen aside. "I can't eat right now."

"Is there anything I can do?"

"Pray the DNA results are negative," she quipped.

"Would it be so terrible to have another brother?" Cassie gently asked. "Family has always been important to you. Look how close you are with Nash, and now you have Skye and Eden."

"What do we truly know about the man? Only what he's chosen to tell us." Her brows collided. "What are you going to do, Cassie? Don't deny you were starting to have feelings for him."

"Go ahead and say I told you so," she said glumly. "I've been naïve. Again."

"Matters of the heart are messy. I should know. I followed a man to Atlanta, even though I had doubts whether he was right for me. Look how that turned out."

In Cassie's opinion, Remi could do better than Patrick Newman. He'd always struck Cassie as arrogant and smug. Of course, as their school's popular, handsome quarterback and son of a prominent attorney, he'd been considered a catch. He and Remi had reconnected several years after graduation and struck up a romance. They'd even gotten engaged.

At least Cassie hadn't let her heart go that far with Luke.

Remi squeezed her shoulder. "Stay with us. My grandparents' old place isn't fancy, but there's an extra bed. Nash and I can keep you safe."

"Luke now has information that suggests my attacker is linked to the deaths of eleven women, not including Hana Moody." Remi's lips parted, and Cassie plunged ahead. "I can't knowingly bring that kind of danger to your doorstep. Nash and Skye have endured enough trouble of their own without having to deal with mine. They should be enjoying their wedding planning. And with little Eden underfoot..." She shook her head. "Besides, I can't leave my animals."

"So you're going to let him stick around?"

"Don't worry, I've learned my lesson. While he's guarding me and my land, I'll be guarding my heart."

THIRTEEN

Cassie managed to keep her distance from Luke the remainder of the weekend, choosing to ride with Remi to church on Sunday and have lunch at the Wilder ranch afterward. She was able to provide emotional support for her friend while avoiding her own inner turmoil. The respite couldn't last forever, however.

On Monday, Luke accompanied her on the FFA field trip to Biloxi. He was quieter than usual, and it felt as if they'd reverted to their previous professional distance. His deception didn't erase his many heroic acts, however, nor the dreamy contentment she'd experienced in his arms on the dance floor.

Jane and Titus, seated in the second-row of her truck, chatted during the entire ride. It was a welcome distraction from the man beside her.

"We're here!" Jane gripped Luke's headrest and peered through the windshield as they turned into the Adventurer RV complex. The January day was a sunny one, with clear blue skies stretching across the horizon.

"What are we having for lunch?" Titus asked. "I'm starving."

Jane laughed at him. "You're always starving."

"Mr. Murphy, the owner, arranged for a barbecue restaurant to cater lunch." Cassie entered the paved circular drive and drove slowly past a modest-size gray warehouse and a collection of new fifth wheels behind a chain-link fence.

Cassie checked her side-view mirrors. Her truck and trailer were the first in their caravan. The other five were either already behind her or in the turning lane. More parents had volunteered to come than ever before, and she guessed it was due to safety concerns.

Temporary fence panels had been set up to form a paddock for their livestock in the central field. On the other side of the circle were two more nondescript warehouses, one substantially larger than the other.

She pointed to the smaller one where people were gathered. "I suppose the luncheon and auction will be in that one."

About fifty RVs were parked off to the side. Mr. Murphy had invited Adventurer club members to participate in this fundraiser event. Cassie estimated there could be one hundred or more people in attendance. She parked between the warehouses and close to the paddock.

Luke perused their surroundings. "How long has Adventurer been a sponsor?"

"Three years. This is the first year we've participated in this sort of event, though. Mr. Murphy is confident it could bring in several thousand dollars. We use donations to buy and repair equipment, to buy animal feed, farm supplies and more. Trips to conventions aren't cheap. We're extremely grateful for our sponsors."

When the trucks and trailers were in their spots, parents and students began spilling into the parking lot. Her students were easily identifiable thanks to their blue corduroy jackets. Each one had the round yellow FFA patch on the back, topped with the name of their state.

Emerging from the truck, Luke cased the area with his astute gaze.

She met him by the hood. "I didn't notice anyone following us, did you?"

"No, but it wouldn't have been hard to blend in with the flow of traffic."

Before leaving school grounds, they'd given the group a reminder to stick together and report anything suspicious.

Please, Lord, let this field trip be a success and protect my students.

Mr. Murphy and his wife greeted them. He informed Cassie that they would split up the group, with half preparing for the livestock presentation and the other half setting up tables and chairs inside. Cassie and Luke remained with the outside group, along with three other adults. Everyone else headed inside with Mr. Murphy.

Cassie caught sight of Morgan and went to help her unload the goats. "Excited for today?"

Morgan's head whipped up, her cheeks blooming with color as she unlatched the trailer gate. She swept her thick braid behind her shoulder. "I guess so."

Cassie helped her lead the goats out of the trailer and into the paddock.

"Are you going to tell my dad about what happened at the dance?" Morgan asked, her voice a mixture of defiance and dread.

"I have serious concerns about you dating a man twelve years older than you. Your dad will share those same concerns."

"You don't know Vince. He treats me like a princess. He's more mature than high school boys."

"He's also the reason you've been distracted in your schoolwork, isn't he? Morgan, you've only got a couple of months left. Look what you've accomplished in a few short years. Don't let that drive and focus slip in the last lap."

She pressed her lips together. "I deserve to have fun, too.

Besides, I—I'm not sure college is right for me after all. I might stay here and get a job in my dad's clinic."

Cassie's jaw dropped. Morgan had worked hard to achieve her goal of attending Ole Miss and becoming a nurse. The university had offered her a generous scholarship.

"Morgan, I'll have to tell your dad about this relationship if you don't. It would be better coming from you."

She gripped her hand. "No, Miss West, you can't. My dad will ground me. He'll forbid me to see Vince! He won't wait for me. He'll find another girl."

"If he's the man God has for you, things will work out. Have you prayed about what God wants for you, Morgan?" she asked gently. "He always knows what is best for us, even when we don't see it."

Or didn't want to. Cassie should've been praying about her relationship with Brian. She'd accepted his proposal without seeking the Lord's will.

"Miss West, can you come over here? Kermit is acting strange."

Cassie glanced over at the girls beside the pig trailer.

"We'll talk about this later."

Farther down the row, Luke was pitching in to help. The teenagers had seen him around enough to accept him, and they included him in their conversations. They even had him laughing. It was a husky sound that squeezed her heart with longing. She turned her attention to Kermit. The pig was much happier outside of his trailer, and the girls breathed a collective sigh of relief.

As soon as the other group finished their task, Mr. Murphy signaled it was time to begin the presentation. Cassie gave her students a pep talk, focusing on the freshmen and sophomores who were newer to the program. Thankfully, her older, more experienced students were good about guiding them and giving pointers. The Adventurer members gathered around the paddock and watched as the students showed their goats and pigs much like they would for an actual competition. The adults were obviously impressed and delighted. Mr. Murphy had given his employees the day off so that they, too, could participate.

Luke, who'd been standing apart from the crowd, joined her. "The kids love this, don't they?"

"Yes. I enjoy watching them learn and mature."

"Will they all go into agricultural-related fields?"

"Some will. Others will take the skills they've gained into other careers."

He lifted his Stetson and ran his fingers through his hair. "I noticed you talking to Morgan. How did that go?"

"I'm worried. She's talking about giving up her dream of becoming a nurse."

"I'd be madder than a puffed toad if Paige had done that."

She let go of the paddock panel. "Do you have a picture of her?"

He scrolled through his phone and angled it toward her. "This is the most recent."

Cassie leaned in, trying not to inhale his tantalizing scent. "She's lovely." The young brunette had a kind smile and sparkling brown eyes.

"She's got a good head on her shoulders. With a protective dad and older brother, she couldn't get into much trouble during high school. Now that she's in college, she's thankfully chosen to focus on her studies. She's on the volleyball team and has found an active Bible study group."

"What's her major?"

"Psychology. She wants to be a child counselor." He showed her another photo. "This is my mom and dad."

Like Paige, Deborah had a kind countenance, and her brown eyes radiated happiness. Ian McCoy had a distinguished air, with strawberry-blond hair and brown eyes.

Luke's eyes had lost their signature guardedness. Now that his secret was out, the protective wall had come down. He was willingly sharing information about his family with her. She would have to keep her own walls in place now.

When the livestock portion was over and the animals sorted, everyone went inside and got in line for the buffet. The tangy, smoky smell of barbecue made her stomach rumble. The students spread out among the tables in order to mingle with the club members and answer questions about the program. Judging from the lively conversations, the event was on its way to being a success. She was incredibly proud of her students.

After lunch, Mr. Murphy explained the auction process while his employees cleared off the tables and brought in more bottled waters and sodas. Cassie and her students jumped in to assist them.

"Miss West?" Maggie, a petite freshman with glasses, rushed up to her. "Jane cut her hand with a serving knife. It's bad."

Cassie hurried over to where the girls had been clearing the buffet tables and assessed the wound. "It doesn't look deep enough for stitches," she said, relieved. "I'll find a first aid kit. Maggie, accompany Jane to the restroom. I'll meet you there."

Cassie stopped the first employee she encountered and explained what happened.

"We have one in the warehouse next door," the young man said. "I'll take you over."

Luke was in deep conversation with a chaperone, Mr. Pasturnak, on the far side of the warehouse. He didn't notice her, and she couldn't take the time to tell him where she was going.

The cool air was welcome after the stuffiness inside. The three giant garage doors of the neighboring warehouse were closed, and her escort led her to the tinted glass door. He pulled it open, only to pause when he heard his name being called.

"Mr. Murphy wants you." His coworker stood near the exit he and Cassie had just used. "He said it's urgent."

The young man shot her an apologetic smile. "The kit is mounted on the wall between the restrooms and vending machines. Straight back on the right. You can't miss it."

He darted off without waiting for her response. Cassie peered into the brightly lit factory and quieted her nerves. She wasn't anywhere near Tulip. It was midday, and there were lots of people around.

Her boot soles were loud against the concrete slab. This warehouse produced fifth wheels, and they were in various stages of production. She zigzagged between raw chassis stacked on top of each other, towers of new tires and machines mounted with rolls of carpet and laminate. A second floor started about halfway back, and she could see an enclosed structure with windows up there. A large sign declared it as the warranty office. Yellow walkways crisscrossed above her head, probably to allow employees to access the RV roofs.

Passing into the space beneath the second floor, she homed in on the glowing vending machines. To her left was a maze of chest-high metal shelving units, all tightly packed with cardboard boxes. She wished she'd thought to ask Mr. Murphy for a tour. The teens would enjoy seeing how RVs were made.

She easily located the first aid kit, but it took her several minutes to release it from its clasps. A moaning sound from deep within the shelves made the hair on the back of her neck stand to attention. Spinning around, she held the rectangular metal box to her chest.

As another painful groan greeted her ears, she worked

up her courage and went to investigate. Her heart leapt into her throat at the sight of a man lying on his back in the middle of an aisle.

"Sir? Can you hear me?"

Crouching beside him, she noticed a gaping wound on his forehead. His eyelids fluttered.

"Help," he whispered.

She touched his forearm. "I'm going to get you help. We need to stop the bleeding first."

Before she could set down the kit and unfasten the lid, his eyes finally opened and focused on her. "Leave."

"I'm not going to leave you. I'll call an ambulance—"

His eyes popped wide. "Leave. Now."

Alarm crawled over Cassie like a hundred tiny spiders.

Out of the corner of her eye, she registered movement. Boxes rained down on them. She tried to shield herself and the injured man. As soon as the onslaught ceased, someone seized her from behind.

Cassie screamed. Swinging the kit upward and out, she caught her attacker in the side of the neck. Grunting in pain, he released her. She scrambled to her feet and knocked boxes out of the way. She dodged pallets and turned into a row of partially assembled campers. Her attacker wasn't wounded, only stunned, and followed closely behind her.

She glanced over her shoulder and tripped over a drain pan. Gasping, she hit the concrete hard, her knees bearing the brunt of her weight. He was bearing down on her. Cassie scrambled on her belly beneath the closest camper. His hands clamped around her boot. She continued toward the opposite side, somehow managing to dislodge him.

He raced around to the other side, blocking her escape. She switched direction. Again, he anticipated her movements. Desperate, Cassie seized the same pan she'd tripped over and shoved it at his ankles with all her might. He cried out. The delay was all she needed to crawl free of the RV.

Unfamiliar with the layout, she wasted precious seconds deciding which way to go. He raced toward her, his eyes promising evil, and she wasn't sure she was getting out alive this time.

FOURTEEN

Terror threatened to render her muscles useless. Although her arms and legs felt weak, Cassie sprinted for the stairs and bounded up to the second floor. She pushed through the swing gate and ran onto a narrow metal walkway suspended high above the factory floor. The gate clanged again as her attacker pursued her with relentless intent.

Now that she up here, she realized it was the wrong choice. The walkway was bolted to the opposite wall but didn't lead anywhere. With her attacker closing in, she had to take drastic action. Ducking beneath the bar into a tight box meant for worker access, she said a prayer and jumped onto an assembled RV.

Cassie landed on the roof and immediately lost her footing on the slippery surface. Arms windmilling, she fell backward and struck her shoulder against the protruding air unit. Her breath stalled in her lungs, and pain rippled through her upper back. There was no time to assess the damage. Above her, the masked man entered the box and prepared to follow her.

She flipped onto her hands and knees and scurried toward the back end. The roof shuddered with the force of his feet striking it. He'd overtake her in a few short strides.

In her haste to get away, she misjudged the distance and slipped over the rounded edge. A scream ripped from her throat. Flailing, she managed to catch the ladder just in time with one hand. Her body swung in mid-air, and she caught the rung with her other hand. Her shoulder throbbed. Before she could climb down safely, he appeared above her. Although his mask covered everything but his eyes, she could almost see his smile of victory. Satisfaction flashed in the dark depths, and wrinkles appeared at the corners.

Her stomach dropped to her toes. He may or may not be a serial killer, but he most certainly relished seeing others in pain. He lifted his foot and shoved it against her fingers, flattening them against the metal.

Cassie cried out. She couldn't hold on. Forced to release the rung, she fell onto the concrete, sprawling on her back. She barely managed to keep her head from whacking against the hard surface. Still, her entire body thrummed with pain.

He took his time climbing down. His assumption that he'd won fueled her with enough energy to roll onto her hands and knees. She gained her feet and hobbled between the campers, gaining strength with each step. Her gaze locked onto a fire alarm mounted on the wall beside a garage door. She had almost reached it when someone rounded a camper and seized her hand.

Luke!

She almost wept with joy. She opened her mouth to speak, and he put his finger to his lips. Guiding her behind the camper, he edged in front of her, lifted his gun and peeked around the side.

Her attacker's advancing footsteps halted abruptly. No one moved. Cassie held her breath.

Luke motioned for her to stay put, then he advanced into the space between the camper they were hiding behind and the next. She shifted to watch his progress, praying for God to intervene and put this to a swift and safe end.

There was a flurry of movement, and Luke raced out of

sight. Ignoring his wishes, she entered the wider aisle as he pursued her assailant deeper into the building. Remembering the injured man, Cassie returned to the last place she'd seen him. She found him there, sitting upright and using the shelves for support. Fear flashed across his face when he saw her approach. She hurried to his side.

"Let's get you out of here," she whispered, leaning down and linking her arm with his. "Can you stand?"

"I think so. I'm feeling lightheaded and weak." He glanced around. "Where is he?"

"My friend went after him. I'm Cassie, by the way. What's your name?"

"Jonathan."

She helped the man to his feet, her own body aching all over. He weaved slightly but caught himself against the shelf. Together, they progressed slowly—too slowly for her peace of mind—toward the exit. She wanted to be clear of this building, out in the daylight and closer to the safety of others.

A door slammed. Cassie halted at the sound of someone running in their direction. When Luke emerged from the production line, she sagged with relief. He was okay. He wasn't returning with her attacker in custody, but he was okay.

"He's gone?" she asked.

"Yes, but we caught a break." Whipping out his phone, he contacted dispatch and rattled off his identity, purpose for calling and the make, model and plate number of the getaway car. He also requested an ambulance. He ended the call and came closer. "Who's this?"

"Jonathan."

"Hi, Jonathan, I'm Luke." He exchanged places with Cassie, and they exited the warehouse together.

Cassie called Mr. Murphy and relayed what had happened. She asked him to keep her students and adult chaperones inside. Shoving her phone back into her pocket, she focused on Jonathan. Luke had helped him to sit on the curb.

"What happened in the warehouse, Jonathan?"

"I work in the warranty office. I had some paperwork to finish up before I could join everyone. I came downstairs and encountered a man wearing a mask. He attacked me before I could confront him."

"What did he hit you with?" Luke gestured to his head wound.

"Large wrench."

Luke turned to Cassie. "I didn't know you were missing until Maggie told me about Jane's hand and that you hadn't returned with the first aid kit."

"I should've told you where I was going." Oh, how she wished she'd taken the spare moment to tell him.

"I'm glad you're okay," he said gruffly.

Reaching over, he gingerly pushed her hair off her forehead. Her breath caught at the intensity of his stare and the brush of his fingers against her skin. Cassie longed to find solace in his arms, to cry out her fear and frustration. She stiffened her spine, determined not to be soft or naïve or foolish with a man ever again.

The police and ambulance arrived together. While the paramedics treated Jonathan, a police officer took her statement. Luke listened, jaw locked and hands fisted, as she relayed her actions step by step.

When the officer had finished his questioning, Luke insisted she go to the hospital. Her shoulder was the most pressing problem. She agreed it was a good idea to get examined. Although reluctant to leave her students, there were enough parents to accompany them safely back to Tulip.

Luke navigated the busy Biloxi streets to the nearest hospital. The emergency room was crowded, and he was full of nervous energy. When he wasn't pacing the room's perimeter, he was perched on the edge of the chair beside her, his knee bouncing and vibrating the entire row.

Noticing the arched stare from the woman across the way, Cassie put her hand on his knee and squeezed. He stilled, his blue eyes cutting to hers and black brows lifting in question.

"How many glasses of sweet tea did you have?" she asked softly.

His gaze darting around, he shifted closer. "I haven't been in a hospital since my surgery."

"Oh." She removed her hand as compassion swelled within her. "Why don't you wait in the truck? I'll be safe here."

"I made the mistake of thinking you'd be safe at the warehouse. I'm sticking to you like glue, Cassidy West."

Her heart flipped over. Why did he have to be so gallant? So handsome? So earnest?

She knew God expected her to forgive him, and she was working on that. But she mustn't let her heart go astray.

He's leaving eventually, she reminded herself. *Don't go wishing he'll fall in love with Tulip. Or with you.*

"Are you sure you're not staying out of guilt?" she said, desperate to fight his hold over her. "Or trying to impress Nash and Remi?"

His chest expanded on a ragged sigh. "I'm staying because I'm not the kind of man who'd run out on a friend when she needed me most."

Friend. Not boss. Not valuable informant. Friend.

Cassie lowered her gaze, picking at the new rip in her jeans. There were bruises forming on her arms and a couple of scratches that hadn't come from working with animals. As much as she hated to admit it, even to herself, she was deeply grateful Luke wasn't hightailing it back to Texas just yet.

Finally, a nurse emerged from the recesses of the ER and called her name. When the woman spied Luke, she frowned.

"I'm her bodyguard," he said. "I go where she goes."

After gaining confirmation from Cassie, the nurse escorted them to an alcove where she monitored her vitals and asked a series of medical questions. They were then directed to a room, where Luke continued to pace like a caged tiger. Was he thinking about his partner and the way he lost him?

"Let's watch television," she suggested.

He lifted his hand to switch on the TV mounted on the wall. His shirt slipped up, revealing scars above his waistband.

Cassie gasped, drawing his attention to her. He grimaced and tugged his shirt down.

"You didn't tell me you suffered burns in that fire."

"It could've been worse," he said. "Much worse."

She was torn between asking him for details of what went down that day and leaving the subject alone. The doctor's arrival saved her from having to make the decision. Luke waited in the hallway while she examined Cassie.

There was a shallow gash and the beginnings of a nasty bruise. The doctor ordered an X-ray, and a nurse cleansed and treated the wound. Luke rejoined her after they'd gone. He'd used the time to update Detective Kane.

There was another knock on the door, and a young sandy-haired orderly came in pushing a wheelchair.

"I'm here to take you to X-ray." He read her wristband information and waited for her to settle in the chair.

He stopped Luke from following them into the hall. "I'm sorry, no visitors are allowed inside the X-ray room. You'll have to wait here."

"I'll wait in the hall outside X-ray," Luke countered, staring down the orderly.

Although flustered, the man didn't argue. He pushed her through a series of short hallways before finally stopping at the destination. Without speaking to Luke, he rolled Cassie inside and closed the door.

"She's here," he called out.

The slight note of uncertainty in his voice caught her attention. Surely she was extra sensitive due to the attacks she'd suffered. Her attacker had fled, and he knew Luke got an eyeful of his getaway car. He wouldn't have waited around to follow them.

Would he?

"I'll be right back," the orderly said and hurried behind the half-wall fitted with protective glass. Cassie heard low voices but couldn't make out the words. She was about to leave when he returned, his face apologetic. Was he flushed? Why wouldn't he meet her gaze?

Was she being paranoid?

"This machine is temperamental. I'm afraid we'll have to use a different one."

He pushed her chair through the opening instead of going back out into the hall. Whoever he'd been speaking with was gone, and there were no other employees around. She didn't like this one bit.

Cassie gripped the armrests. "I need to go to the bathroom. Is there one nearby?"

"This won't take long."

He pushed her into another X-ray room and backed away without speaking. The door closing was like the lid of a coffin snapping shut.

Cassie put her feet on the floor and stood up. She wasn't sticking around.

A connecting door opened, and a man in blue scrubs

and a surgical mask entered the room. The first thing she noticed was his eyes. The second was the slim leather belt hanging from his hand.

"You're not getting away this time, Cassie."

FIFTEEN

Every minute in this sterile bunker ate at Luke's peace of mind. He kept the memories at bay with prayer. He'd endured plenty of nightmares in the weeks and months after Simon's death—waking up in a cold sweat, heart racing and disoriented, the stench of fire and burning flesh as real as if he were still trapped in that garage. Nothing helped ease the residual fear and grief like talking to God.

Once again faced with unpleasant thoughts, he prayed for his parents and Paige, Hersh, Amber and their unborn baby, his coworkers, Nash, Skye, Eden and Remi. Lastly, he prayed for Cassie. He asked God to keep His hand of protection on her and to help her work through the emotional and physical toll of these ongoing attacks.

A man and woman in scrubs turned the corner and quickly approached him. He recognized the nurse who'd tended to Cassie's shoulder wound.

"Excuse me, you're here with Cassie West, aren't you? Scott came to her room to take her to X-ray, and it was empty. Have you seen her?"

Luke's heart slowed. "She's already in X-ray." He pointed to the door opposite.

"I'm the only one on shift right now," the orderly said. "Everyone else is on break." He knocked on the door Luke had indicated before entering. "She's not here."

Luke brushed past him. "Cassie?"

The dimly lit room contained only a chair, bed and X-ray machine. He dashed into the employees' area. "Cassie!"

"Sir, you can't be back here," the orderly called after him.

Luke dashed from room to room, his heart sinking a little more each time he was greeted by empty space. He was almost to the end of the corridor when he heard a thump. Bursting into the room on his right, he saw Cassie slumped on the floor. Light spilled in through the other door linked to a high-traffic hallway. Her eyes were closed.

His whole body went cold. *Not again, Lord.*

Dropping to the floor, he checked her throat for a pulse. He breathed a sigh of relief at the steady, strong rhythm.

"What's going on?" The nurse and orderly barged in behind him, only to stop short.

"Contact security," he ordered, carefully taking her limp body into his arms. "Tell them to lock down the building. Search the parking lot for a 2002 black Honda Civic. The man who attacked her had an accomplice." Luke rattled off the particulars of the fake orderly.

He cradled her head against his shoulder. "Cassie? Can you hear me?"

There were no ligature marks on her throat. She hadn't been strangled. Could he have sedated her? Poisoned her?

While the nurse spoke with hospital security on the phone, the orderly went to fetch a doctor.

Cassie stirred. "Luke?"

Her lashes fluttered open, and she stared at him uncomprehendingly.

"It's okay, Cass. I've got you. You're safe."

Gradually, her confusion cleared. Her eyes widened. She gripped his forearm. "He was here. Luke, he spoke to me."

The fact that this man broke his own rule of silence—not to mention coming after her when authorities were already searching for his vehicle—painted a disturbing picture. He was getting desperate. Whether that would work in their favor or not remained to be seen.

"I'm going to help you up now." He looped an arm beneath her knees and scooped her up. She clung to him. "I've got you." He settled her on the X-ray bed and sat on the edge. "How are you feeling?"

"Lightheaded. He didn't touch me, though. He spoke to me. He said I wasn't getting away this time. I heard you calling for me. He was running out the door when my vision went fuzzy. I must've blacked out."

"I heard a noise and came inside. That must've been you hitting the floor."

Reaching over, he gingerly explored her scalp. Her gaze was locked on his, and he felt a frisson of awareness pass between them.

A security guard arrived and introduced himself as Mike Lang. "My guys are searching for the orderly and the car. You don't have a description of the perpetrator?"

Luke looked to Cassie.

"He was wearing blue scrubs, a surgical hat and mask. His eyebrows are black and thick. His eyes are dark. Brown, I think."

"Did you notice his shoes? Tattoos or scars on his arms? Jewelry?" Luke prompted.

"He had those disposable covers on his shoes. He was also wearing a white long-sleeved shirt under the scrubs and exam gloves on his hands."

The security guard pointed under the bed. "What's that?"

Luke bent to look and received a shock. "I need an evidence bag."

Cassie slowly sat up. "What is it?"

"A slim black leather belt."

She shook her head. "He's too smart to leave fingerprints."

"It can still be useful."

The guard left, presumably to get the evidence bag. The doctor arrived, and after declaring her vitals normal, he listened to their account of everything that had occurred that day.

"What did you have to eat today?"

Cassie had skipped breakfast and admitted to only picking at her lunch.

"Are you prone to low blood sugar?"

"Not that I'm aware of."

"It could be that the lack of nutrients, coupled with the shocking events, caused you to faint. I'm not too concerned since you weren't out long. However, I recommend you take a few days off work and get some rest. If you have any changes in vision or headaches or any unusual symptoms, seek medical attention right away. You should also follow up with your primary physician."

After the doctor had gone, Cassie finally got an X-ray and was cleared of any fractures. They went to the hospital security office in search of Mike Lang. He informed them that Biloxi PD had arrived and were reviewing security footage. They were also scouring the parking lots and surrounding streets for the Honda Civic. Unfortunately, they hadn't been able to locate the man disguised as a hospital orderly.

Luke was reluctant to leave until the officers finished their search. At his insistence, Cassie agreed to eat something. He bought her a bowl of tomato soup and a tuna sandwich at the cafeteria. Finding a booth in the corner, he sat with his back to the wall, nursing a cup of black coffee and trying not to fidget.

After eating half of the tray's contents, she pushed it to the side. "I can't eat any more."

"Is the lightheadedness gone?"

"I feel much better." She crushed her paper napkin into a ball. "There's no reason I can't go to work tomorrow."

"I'm siding with the doctor on this one. You've been through a lot in recent days. To tell you the truth, I'm surprised Gabriela hasn't ordered you to take time off."

"It's not as easy as you might think to get a substitute for ag classes."

"You've gone through significant trauma. You have to consider your mental health."

Her heavily lashed brown eyes studied him. "Is that what your extended leave is for?"

He drained his coffee. "That's a complicated question. I don't know if I'll ever get over Simon's death."

Her forehead furrowed. "You told me not to blame myself for my attacker's actions. The same applies to you. I read the news coverage. You and Simon were targets of a powerful criminal."

Gritting his teeth, he rubbed at a coffee stain on his jeans. He'd heard the same message from almost everyone in his life...fellow officers, family and friends. Even Stella, Simon's wife, had begged him not to assume the burden of Simon's passing. It was different coming from Cassie.

"Oleg Sokolov had been on our radar for some time. He was responsible for a pipeline of heroin and fentanyl into our city. He got greedy and started selling tainted supplies, causing dozens of deaths. Many of them were minors. Simon and I decided to go after him. We built the case from the ground up, starting with low-level dealers and flipping them for bigger and bigger fish. We finally reached Sokolov's second in command, who agreed to testify against his boss in exchange for immunity. There was a leak, though. Sokolov ordered an informant to lure us to that garage. We'd met him there many times and didn't think anything of it." He stared across the cafeteria, unseeing.

The whisper of her fingers curling around his jolted him back to the present. She looked sad. "It was a trap."

"Yeah." He cleared his throat and, staring at their joined hands, rubbed his thumb over hers. Her skin was cool and soft. "Our informant slipped outside, closed the doors and wedged them shut. They were metal and impenetrable. He threw a Molotov cocktail through a window. The old building was packed with junk and cardboard boxes full of clothes, newspapers and who knows what else. The flames ate that stuff up. It was fast. Too fast for us to reach the windows, which were high, almost to the ceiling."

She increased the pressure. "Oh, Luke. I can't imagine."

"Time has helped a little. I had nightmares in the beginning. They aren't as frequent now."

"Did you see a counselor?"

"I couldn't bring myself to talk about it. I plan to see someone when I return to Texas, though."

She lowered her gaze and removed her hand.

"I did talk to my pastor a few times," he continued. "My friend and coworker, Hersh, became my accountability partner."

"What do your friends and family think about your decision to come here?"

"They're worried about me, especially my mom. I'm afraid this has brought old hurts to the surface. Ian understands my need for answers. He also understands that he's my dad and always will be, no matter that we're not blood related. He's trying to support us both."

"It sounds like you were raised by wonderful people. As painful as Wes's rejection has been, it was most likely a blessing in disguise. Nash and Remi didn't have it easy after Glory's death. Wes provided for them, but he was a difficult man."

Her phone pinged. She read the text and some of the tightness in her expression eased. "The students arrived safely at school and the animals are tucked in." Another text came in. "Gabriela wants to speak to me."

Cassie made the call, her defeated tone revealing the gist of the conversation.

"Gabriela strongly encouraged me to take the rest of the week off."

Luke couldn't hide his relief. Cassie would be safer on the ranch where he could keep an eye on her. He prayed the belt would be the key to unmasking this guy at last.

Cassie couldn't forget yesterday's horror. Her whole body was sore, especially her shoulder. She looked forward to a long soak in the bath after brushing down Buck. In the next stall over, Luke hummed along with the radio, occasionally singing the words. His voice was clear and smooth, and he sang on tune. His presence was a comfort, despite her tumultuous feelings about him.

At the sound of an approaching vehicle, she started for the open door. Luke intercepted her, his pistol drawn and his eyes shouting a warning. He exited first and peered down the gravel drive.

He holstered his weapon. "It's Evan and Arianna. Were you expecting them?"

"She mentioned they might stop by after school."

Had Morgan finally come clean about Vince?

Returning the brush to the shelf, she watched the pair exit Evan's truck. The sticker on his door advertised his veterinary clinic and services. He smiled across at Arianna, came around the hood and held out his hand. Arianna's face radiated happiness.

The couple's mood suggested they were still in the dark about Morgan's dating life.

* * *

After greeting Luke with a handshake, Evan and Arianna took turns hugging Cassie.

"We're so glad you're all right." Arianna's emerald-green eyes filled with worry.

"I'm glad the kids didn't witness any of it." Cassie looked at Evan. "Did Morgan say anything?"

He shrugged. "Not much. Morgan's been quieter than usual lately, though. I think she's stressed about the upcoming ACT exam and the reality of what happens after graduation."

Cassie wrestled with what to do. She'd hoped Morgan would come clean with her father. Should she give her more time? Cassie taught teenagers, but she didn't have the experience or skills of a parent.

Evan deserved to know the truth. Keeping quiet felt deceitful. Thanks to Luke, she knew how it felt to be blindsided by a secret. Guilt churning in her middle, Cassie bit her lip. Would her sharing this news make Morgan more determined to be with Vince? Would she do something drastic? She was eighteen, after all. She could pack her things and leave.

Arianna reached up to pick a hair off Evan's sweater, and Cassie caught sight of her new accessory.

She clapped her hand over her mouth. "You're engaged?"

Arianna's cheeks pinked. "Since last night."

Evan put his arm around Arianna. "She finally said yes."

She held out her hand so that Cassie could inspect the ring.

"It's beautiful," Cassie said. "When's the big day?"

"Late July."

"Congratulations." Luke and Evan shook hands.

"We wanted to have time to celebrate Morgan's graduation before the whirlwind weeks before the ceremony."

Arianna tucked her hair behind her ear. "We also wanted to schedule it before she heads off to college."

"That makes sense." Her guilt returned. They assumed Morgan was still planning to attend MSU. They didn't know she was thinking of skipping college altogether.

"We didn't come to discuss the wedding," Arianna stated. "We're here to check on you."

"Arianna insisted we swing by the bakery on our way here. She bought lemon iced cookies to make you feel better," Evan told Cassie, his eyes twinkling. "There are two dozen in the truck."

Cassie's brows rose, and she turned to Luke. "I hope you like lemon, because you're going to have to help me eat them."

Luke smiled. "As it so happens, I do."

"Thank you, Arianna," Cassie said. "That was thoughtful."

"I'm worried about you. Have the Biloxi police made any headway in finding your attacker?"

"They found his getaway vehicle abandoned on a side street near the hospital. It turned out to be stolen. They're scouring it for trace evidence."

She didn't mention the belt or their theory he'd killed before. Detective Kane didn't want that information shared.

Arianna clung to Cassie's hand. "I'm praying every day."

"Prayer is what keeps me going." She nodded toward the open door. "Why don't you both come in for coffee?"

"We'd love to, but Evan's got a patient to see in the next county over. I'm going with him." She tugged on her hand. "Let's get those cookies for you."

Evan talked with Luke while Cassie followed Arianna to the truck. "What made you decide to accept his proposal?" she asked quietly. "I thought you had reservations."

Arianna retrieved a white pastry box. "I love Evan. At the end of the day, he's the only one I can see myself with."

Cassie searched her friend's face for misgivings. "You're sure?"

"Positive. He makes me happy." She passed the box to Cassie, and the scent of lemon and sugar made her mouth water. "What about you and Luke?"

"What about us?"

"Is there any chance you'll forgive him?"

She could see him through the barn's open door, looking handsome without much effort at all. He looked like he belonged on the West ranch. Her heart beat with yearning.

"I've already forgiven him." After all, her heavenly Father had forgiven her, and she was supposed to show that same grace to others. "But we don't have a future together."

Would she even have a future? Her usual positive outlook had become tarnished in recent weeks, and her future was shrouded in gloomy uncertainty. Cassie was losing hope that they'd ever identify her would-be killer. Luke couldn't stay here forever. He'd get tired of the danger eventually, and he'd return to Texas.

Would he take her heart and her chance of survival with him?

SIXTEEN

Cassie entered the Mayfield City Police Department that evening with knots in her belly. Detective Kane had been mysterious about his reasons for summoning them, and her mind whirled with possibilities. She prayed there hadn't been another victim.

They were directed upstairs to a large open space containing multiple desks. There was an enclosed office in the far corner and a breakroom beside it. At this time of night, the desks were empty. Remi was still on duty, however. She emerged from the break room with a sandwich in one hand and a soda in the other.

"Kane had to run downstairs. He won't be long."

Perching on the corner of her desk, she set the soda on top of her desk calendar. Her expression was guarded, and Cassie was pretty sure it was because of Luke. They hadn't yet received the results from the DNA test.

"You don't happen to know what he's brought us here for, do you?" she asked.

Her brow creased. "I wish I did." She popped up and opened the door to the office. "You can wait in here. Do either of you want coffee?"

"I'll take some," Luke said.

"Be right back."

Kane's office looked like a toddler had put his hands into

every pile. Cassie quickly forgot that when she noticed the corkboard on the wall behind the desk. Photographs of the killer's victims were pinned to the board, along with their names and ages. The blond-haired, brown-eyed women smiled at her. The lemon cookies she'd eaten earlier threatened to come up.

Luke's touch startled her. He stood close, his hand on her shoulder. His eyes were sympathetic.

"You're not alone in this."

Remi breezed inside and handed Luke a Styrofoam cup. Noticing the board, she grimaced. "I know this is hard, Cass. Maybe Kanc has had a breakthrough."

At least Jim Hallman had been cleared as a suspect. After the dance, Kane had gone to the Hallman residence. Not only was Tracy alive and well, Jim had a solid alibi for all but one of Cassie's attacks.

Kane returned, sidestepped Remi and sank into his rolling desk chair. "Thank you both for coming. Have a seat."

Remi left the office, closing the door behind her. The air felt chilled. Once seated in the hard plastic chair, she rubbed her hands together. "Did your team find evidence in the Honda Civic? What about the belt? Do you know who he is yet?"

Kane leaned back in his chair. "They're still examining the vehicle. As for the belt, there weren't any fingerprints."

Luke balanced the cup on his knee. "Have you looked into the manufacturer and local stores that sell that particular brand? That might lead to security footage or a credit card receipt."

"We're exploring that angle." He shifted the haphazard pile of papers on his desk and picked up a sticky note. "The belt was made in Scotland."

"Scotland?" Cassie met Luke's gaze. "That should make the sellers easier to narrow down."

"Unless it was purchased online," Luke responded.

"As a matter of fact, I've tracked it to a specialty shop in Biloxi. It's in a complex that caters to tourists."

Cassie leaned forward. "Have you spoken to the owner?"

He nodded. "She's agreed to meet with me. I'm heading down there tomorrow morning."

Hope sparked inside her. This was the best lead they'd had yet.

"Did the hospital capture any footage?" Luke asked. "We need to find that orderly."

"As a matter of fact, that's why I asked you to come." He picked up a pair of folders. "I'd like each of you to study the photographs inside and tell me if anyone looks familiar. Please don't consult with each other."

Cassie's heart pounded as she opened the folder and examined the document with photos of six different men. She didn't have to look long. She held it out to Kane and tapped the middle bottom photo. "This one."

He jotted down a note and waited for Luke's response. Once he'd pointed out the suspect, Kane smiled. "You identified the same man. His name is Carl Jenkins, and he's known to the Biloxi PD for the occasional misdemeanor. We didn't get a recording of him with Cassie, but we did see him hurrying from an exit close to the X-ray area. The hospital confirmed he isn't an employee."

Cassie felt like breaking into a dance. "This is even better than the belt," she said, unable to contain her excitement. "Are you going to arrest him?"

"I'll contact Biloxi to scoop him up. I'll have a chat with him after I speak to the shop owner."

"A chat? What does that mean exactly? Luke and I have identified him as the man who did the killer's bidding."

Luke touched her arm. "We don't want him for impersonating a hospital employee. We need him to give us information about the man who hired him."

Kane agreed. "I'll offer him whatever I can in order to get him to cooperate."

Her excitement ebbed. "You'll let us know what you find out?"

"Yes, ma'am."

She looked at the women on the board again. "I pray they get justice."

"Have you figured out his motive?" Luke said.

Kane rotated his chair and studied the board. "We haven't been able to establish a connection between these women other than their looks and age."

"He could be someone who needs to exert control," Luke mused. "Although Hana Moody's murder suggests he picks his victims at random, that doesn't fit with his fixation with Cassie. On top of that, he's starting to take risks. He used an accomplice this time, which puts him at risk for discovery, and he spoke to Cassie for the first time."

Cassie grimaced. "I was focused on survival, not trying to recognize his voice."

"Has he shown a pattern? Left a memento or taken a trophy?"

Kane frowned. "Each victim had a chunk of her hair sheared off."

Goose bumps dimpled Cassie's arms. This man was sick and twisted, and he wanted her to be his next victim. She didn't track Luke's and Kane's next statements as she thought about the victims and their families. Cassie was glad her parents weren't in town. They would be beside themselves with worry. Not only that, but they could accidentally get caught up in the violence. So far, Luke had escaped harm, and she thanked God for it.

Kane stood and gestured to the door. "I'll contact you with any developments."

Remi wasn't anywhere to be seen when they emerged from the office. Outside in the truck, the heater on full blast, Luke turned off the radio and stretched his arm along the seat.

"They're making progress," he said. "That's something to be thankful for."

"I guess."

"I'm proud of you, you know. I've worked with people who crumbled under much less pressure. You're strong. You'll get through this."

She clasped her hands in her lap. "It's not my strength. It's God's. If He wasn't my foundation, my source of comfort and peace, I probably wouldn't leave my house."

He picked at a rip in the seat seam. "Truth is, I've been trying to handle my grief and guilt over Simon's death on my own when I should've been seeking God's help. Thanks for the reminder that I need to rely on Him and not myself."

"I'm glad you wound up on my ranch," Cassie admitted. "I'm glad you stayed."

Surprise rippled across his angular features.

Feeling exposed, Cassie shifted her gaze to the police station building. "The pot roast I left in the slow cooker will be a hunk of charcoal if we don't get home soon."

"To be honest, I'm not hungry after all those cookies."

Cassie smiled. "You did eat more than your fair share."

When they drove down her driveway half an hour later, his headlights skimmed over a Volkswagen with Texas plates parked at her parents' house.

Luke tapped the brakes. "I don't believe this."

Cassie's gaze swung between his unhappy face and the young brunette slipping from the driver's side. Unhappiness shot through her as she wondered if this was a girlfriend he'd neglected to mention.

"Who is that, Luke?"

He threw the truck into park and switched off the ignition. "My sister."

As motion lights flickered on, Cassie recognized her from the photo he'd showed her. Paige's delicate features were wreathed in happy expectation. Luke, on the other hand, looked like a bank of storm clouds about to unleash their fury.

Leaving the truck, he stalked around the hood, his gaze scanning the barn and outbuildings and dark fields. "What are you doing here, Paige?"

She huddled in her thick overcoat. "I'm here to see you, of course."

Cassie shut her passenger door and watched the siblings' exchange with fascination. Where Luke was big and brawny, Paige was petite. The top of her head barely reached his chin.

He threaded his fingers through his hair. "You shouldn't have come."

"Why not?" Her smile wobbled. "I missed you."

"Let's go inside." Taking her elbow, he marched her to the front door.

"Aren't you going to introduce me to your boss?" She glanced over her shoulder.

Cassie gave her a commiserating smile before turning to greet Dusty, who trotted out of the shadows. Once they were all inside, Luke told them to stay put while he did a quick sweep.

After closing and locking the door, Cassie stuck out her hand. "Hi. I'm Cassie West."

"Nice to meet you. Sorry for showing up on your doorstep unannounced, but my brother's been gone a while. I've been worried about him." She let Dusty sniff her hand before gingerly stroking his back. The dog ate up her attention as if they'd known each other forever.

Luke strode between the couch and entertainment center. "You should've called. Driving here all alone without telling me—" He shook his head in exasperation. "How many times have I stressed safety?"

"Too many to count. I'm not a child, Luke McCoy, so stop treating me like one." Paige pressed her lips together. "I thought you'd be happy to see me. Guess I was mistaken."

She pivoted toward the door. The starch went out of Luke, and he reached for her, his fingers snagging her coat. "Paige, wait. I'm sorry."

Paige turned around, flipping her brown hair behind her shoulder.

"I'm very happy to see you." He wrapped his arms around her, and she rested her head against his chest. "I was worried, that's all."

Cassie wanted to stay and see more of this tender side of Luke. Instead, she removed her jacket and stepped toward the coat closet. "I'll give you some privacy."

Paige stepped out of his arms. "Please stay. Luke isn't the best of communicators under normal circumstances, never mind text messaging. He's been frustratingly tightlipped about his time here. I was hoping you can fill in any gaps."

Cassie arched a brow at him. "Trust me, I'm aware of his tendency to keep things to himself."

Luke grimaced.

"Annoying, isn't it?" Paige nudged him.

"It has its drawbacks."

Luke felt like a bug under a microscope.

Paige smirked up at him. "You didn't mention that your boss is young *and* beautiful."

Cassie choked on a laugh. "I'll be in the kitchen."

Dusty followed her and waited near the treat jar. She rewarded his obvious request with several small treats before hurriedly assembling snacks for the adults.

Luke shrugged out of his jacket and held his hand out for Paige's. "Don't you have classes this week?"

She gave him her coat and glanced around, her curiosity plain. "I only have classes on Mondays, Wednesdays and Fridays. Two are online, and another was canceled for the rest of the week because my professor went into labor. The sub will step in starting Monday. My laptop's in the car. As long as there's decent Wi-Fi, I can stick around until Saturday."

His insides locked up. While he had missed his little sister, he didn't want her anywhere near Tulip. Just being around him and Cassie put Paige in danger.

Cassie carried a tray into the living room and set it on the coffee table. "Help yourself." She pointed to the arrangement of leftover lemon cookies, fruit, crackers and cheese. "Would you like coffee or hot chocolate?"

"Water's fine, thanks." Paige snagged an apple, took a big bite and got comfortable on the couch.

Luke sat down beside her. "Do Mom and Dad know you're here?"

"I called Dad once I was on the road and left a message. I should probably text him." She balanced the apple on her knee and typed a quick text.

"What about Mom?"

"I got her voicemail, too."

That explained why he hadn't been warned. His parents were aware of the danger and would be very worried about her.

Cassie placed some bottles beside the tray, took one for herself and sat on the loveseat.

Paige touched his arm. "How's your shoulder?" She turned to Cassie. "He did tell you about that, right?"

Twisting the bottle between her palms, Cassie's expression became guarded. "Yes, he did."

"It's holding up," he said, grateful Cassie hadn't mentioned his duplicity. "Getting stronger every day."

"How did Luke come to work for you?"

"Well, our downtown café is our town's communication center, and he heard I needed a ranch hand while my parents are in Florida."

"A dream for Luke. He enjoyed helping on our uncle's farm." She gestured to the windows. "I couldn't see much of your ranch as I drove in. Will you take me on a tour?"

Cassie smiled. "Tomorrow's supposed to be nice. We can take the horses or the four-wheeler."

"Horses for sure. I'm a Texas gal, after all. How long has your family lived here?"

"My whole life. I could ride before I could walk, my dad likes to say. I can't imagine living anywhere else."

"Texas has its charms, too," Paige said, cutting Luke a sly look. "You should come for a visit. My parents live in a typical suburban neighborhood, but Luke owns several acres outside of town. He's planning to buy horses as soon as he gets fences installed."

Cassie's brows lifted. "Is that so?"

Paige grinned up at him. "You'd welcome a chance to show her around, wouldn't you?"

He knew where this was headed and tried to cut her off. "Cassie's an agriculture teacher at the local high school."

"Really? Our county has an active FFA group. It's one of the largest in the state. There's always a need for ag teachers."

Cassie bit her lip, and her eyes danced. "Do you plan to stay in the San Antonio area after graduation?"

The women launched into a discussion of Paige's post-college plans. Luke watched their exchange with interest, not surprised they had an almost instant rapport. Of course his sister would like Cassie. Who wouldn't?

She was his ideal woman. For the first time in his life, he could picture a specific woman as his life partner. Unfortunately, she'd seen the worst of him. Sure, she'd forgiven him, and she was willing to trust him with her life. Her heart and happiness were another matter.

Disappointment and—dare he say hurt?—threatened to swallow him whole.

Surely he hadn't done something foolish like fall in love with her?

Cassie covered a yawn, and Paige nudged him. "We've overstayed our welcome. I brought a sleeping bag. Or is there an extra bed in your apartment?"

Luke frowned, and Cassie's face lost its animation.

Paige's gaze bounced between them, her brows tugging together. "Is there a problem?"

Luke had tried to protect his sister from the harsher side of life and the violence that he saw on a regular basis. But he couldn't keep her in the dark about this.

She sighed. "You two can stop with the silent communication. Something's obviously wrong."

Luke put his hand on her shoulder. "The truth is, Paige, it isn't safe for you to be here."

"Why not?"

He caught Cassie's gaze. She slowly nodded.

"Cassie has become a target of a serial killer."

SEVENTEEN

"This is terrible." Paige sank onto the foot of the guest bed. "Poor Cassie."

Even though the primary bedroom was on the other side of the house, Luke closed the door. Cassie had endured the retelling of her circumstances yet again. She didn't need to hear him and his sister discussing it further.

He tugged the chair from beneath the desk, flipped it around and straddled it, resting his forearms on the top rung. His exhaustion was more mental than anything.

"Luke, just think… You came here to meet your siblings, but God had a bigger purpose. You showed up at the exact time Cassie needed protection. I mean, you're a cop. Who better to protect her than you?"

He stared at his sister. The idea hadn't occurred to him.

She spread her hands. "What if she hadn't found anyone to help on the ranch? She would've been alone."

Luke vividly remembered the night the killer almost breached Cassie's tiny home. A chill passed through him. The outcome might've been very different if she'd been by herself.

"You understand now why you have to go home tomorrow morning," he stated.

"Cassie said she's off for the rest of the week. That means you guys will be staying on the ranch, right? I'd either be inside studying or roaming the property with you two. That's safe."

He remembered when he hadn't yet developed a healthy respect for danger. Like Paige, he'd considered himself invincible. "Not safe enough."

Sorrow slithered through her eyes, taking him unawares. "You don't understand what it was like for us in the wake of your accident. You shut us out. We wanted to help, but you refused to be helped. It hurt. A lot. And then you took off on this mysterious trip and got a job… I've been wondering if you're ever coming home."

"Of course I'm coming home." He leaned forward and held out his hand. Paige placed hers atop his and lifted her puppy dog eyes. "You're right, I have no idea what you, Mom and Dad went through. I was self-absorbed and oblivious to your feelings. I'm sorry."

"I want to spend some time with you. I also want to meet the Wilders. What are they like?"

"Remi is spunky, smart as a whip and fiercely loyal to those in her inner circle. Nash is complicated. He's a family man and a hard worker. Both are well-liked and respected by the locals. Because they consider Cassie part of their family, they've kept their guard up around me. They're protective of her." He shrugged. "They were right to be suspicious. I hid my identity from everyone."

Her brows hit her hairline. "From Cassie, too?"

Shame engulfed him. He was supposed to set a good example. "I was too focused on my own objectives to think about how my deception would impact her."

"You didn't know you'd grow to care about her."

Her insight reminded him that Paige wasn't a little girl anymore. She was a young woman on the cusp of forging her future.

When he didn't deny it, she said, "Cassie seems like a

caring, compassionate woman. I'm sure she'll get past it. After all, I sensed a strong connection between the two of you."

That connection was tied to the danger they found themselves in. Standing, he returned the chair to its spot. "Get some rest, sis. You've got a long trip ahead of you."

Paige stood and crossed her arms. "I'm staying until Saturday."

Luke recognized the flare of stubbornness and acknowledged he couldn't physically propel her off the property. A knock on the door distracted him.

"Sorry to interrupt." Cassie's hair was a rippling blond river past her shoulders, and she wore blue pajamas with cartoon yetis. Her face was dewy and free of makeup, and he was tempted to brush his thumb over her full bottom lip to test its softness.

"I just got a call from Remi. The DNA results came in, and she and Nash would like to see you tomorrow."

His heart squeezed. "And?"

"It's as you said. You're a Wilder."

"You're worried about him, aren't you?"

Paige traipsed through the damp field behind Cassie the next morning. Howard Beineke, owner of a neighboring ranch, was missing three cows. A low-lying creek bordered their properties, and cattle would occasionally wander between the ranches. After wolfing down breakfast, she, Luke and Paige had driven to the back pasture. Luke was checking on another group of cattle, within sight but out of hearing range.

Cassie stopped and turned. "Is it that obvious?"

Paige was proving to be an insightful young woman. Cassie had taken an instant liking to Luke's younger sister. She was lively, friendly and sweet.

Paige studied her. "You two obviously care about each other." Her mouth curved in a lazy half smile that mimicked her brother's. "He's going to be okay. I wouldn't have been able to say that a few months ago. Being here with you was exactly what he needed to heal. Guess you both benefited from his arrival."

Hiring Luke, getting to know him, being protected by him... Her life would forever be changed.

"I hope the Wilders don't impede the progress he's made," she tacked on.

"They're good people," Cassie said quietly. "They simply don't know him like you do."

Like I do.

"They'd better give him a chance, or they'll have me to answer to," Paige huffed.

Paige obviously adored her big brother. Seeing the two together increased her curiosity about his life in Texas. She refrained from voicing her burning questions so as not to give Paige more reason to tease Luke.

Something bumped her from behind, and she turned and greeted the big blond cow. "Hey there, Blondie."

"Is she a special friend?"

Cassie gently rubbed the cow's head. "I bottle-fed her when she was a baby. My dad's had opportunities to sell her, but he's kept her around for me."

"He sounds like a softie."

"When it comes to his only child, he is."

Paige smiled and glanced around, admiring the fields stretching to the horizon. "I thought Luke would take up farming after he graduated high school. I was surprised when he chose law enforcement."

"He knows his way around a ranch." Probably why she hadn't questioned his reasons for being in Tulip. Funny, the sting of his deception wasn't quite what it used to be. "Why did he become a cop?"

"He wanted to help people and make a positive difference in our community. He's really good at what he does." Her shoulders slumped. "He and Simon were a great team."

"How long were they partners?"

"Four years. Simon and his wife, Stella, were like my adopted uncle and aunt. Our families dropped by each other's houses unannounced and celebrated milestones together. Simon's greater police experience balanced Luke's spot-on instincts. They were in perfect sync, and they had each other's backs. The way we lost Simon was tough to process. It was a shock for us all, and to come so close to losing Luke..." Her eyes filled with tears, and she quickly blinked them away.

Cassie could only imagine how Paige and her parents must've felt...much like Cassie would feel if something were to happen to Nash or Remi. How she would feel if Luke got hurt protecting her...

"He's in danger again because of me."

Paige studied her brother as he strode through the field toward them, his gaze shadowed by the brim of his Stetson. "It's not easy knowing he risks his life every day to protect others, but I wouldn't ask him to change."

"Protecting me isn't part of his job description."

Paige looked at her, curiosity in her eyes. "No one's forcing him to."

Luke joined them and patted Blondie. "I didn't see Howard's animals."

A cold breeze teased her hair, and she regretted not bringing a heavier coat. "They're possibly in the west pasture."

Luke shrugged out of his coat and placed it around Cassie's shoulders.

Paige smiled knowingly as Cassie murmured her thanks

and tugged the heavy coat lapels together. His heat and scent enveloped her, but they were a poor substitute for his strong arms.

As they made their way back to the truck, Luke shot her a glance. "Have you considered getting a drone?"

"I've talked to my dad about it. He's resistant to change. Nash has one, and he said it's made certain tasks easier."

"Like locating naughty cows," Paige piped up.

Cassie and Luke exchanged a smile. The intimacy of it curled her toes in her boots.

After checking the west pasture, she let Howard know they'd found his cows. He promised to come by and pick them up within the hour. The rest of the morning flew by, and they were soon climbing back into the truck to make the short drive to Nash and Remi's.

When they arrived, Cassie rested her hand on the passenger door handle. "You're sure you don't want to go in alone? Paige and I can wait in the barn. The ranch hands could keep us company."

While they weren't cops, Nash's ranch hands knew their way around a rifle and were a tough lot.

"Remi will want you there," he said. "I do, too."

Once inside, Luke introduced Nash, Remi and Skye to Paige. They hovered awkwardly in the foyer, and the tension was thick and uncomfortable. Cassie didn't know whether to hug Remi or remain by Luke's side.

"Where's Eden?" Cassie finally asked.

"She's with a sitter." Skye stood very close to Nash, her hand on his back. "We thought it would be best."

Remi cleared her throat and gestured to the kitchen. "Would anyone like pie? Coffee?"

Paige perked up. "I never turn down pie."

Seemingly oblivious, Paige skirted the others and helped herself from the spread on the bar. No one else made a move. Remi's arms formed a defensive shield over her middle, and she shifted from one foot to the other. Cassie could count on one hand the number of times she'd seen her friend like this.

She closed the distance between them and squeezed her hand. "I've been praying for you. For all of you."

Remi gave her a solemn smile.

"Have a seat," Nash said, and then he and Skye led the way into the living room.

The couple settled on the couch. Luke and Cassie took the stuffed floral chairs on either side of the coffee table. Remi lowered herself onto the cushion beside Skye. Paige trailed in and remained standing, scooping in quick bites.

"Why are you all acting like this is a funeral? You have a new family member. That's something to celebrate," she said.

Luke shot his sister a meaningful glance before shifting to the edge of his seat. "I want to reiterate that I don't have expectations of you. I'm not after an inheritance. I'll be returning to Texas eventually." He rubbed his hands on his jeans. "I simply want to get to know my biological father's side of the family. I'd like to learn about my heritage."

Cassie's insides knotted at his words. The reaction didn't make sense. She knew Luke had a life to go back to. She knew it was for the best.

Remi spoke first. "That's fair. It's difficult for us to accept that our father betrayed our mother. He was a harsh man with impossible standards. I think Nash will agree that his love for our mother was his one redeeming character trait. To have that ripped away…" She pressed her lips together.

Nash rested his forearms on his knees and looked Luke square in the eye. "I don't like the way you went about this whole thing. However, I respect the way you've stuck by

Cassie when you didn't have to. Remi's right. Our father's affair adds another layer of difficulty to an already complicated matter. It makes me sick to think of the pain he might've caused Mom. We don't know if she ever found out."

"He hurt my mom, too," Luke inserted.

Nash inclined his head. "I'm sorry that she, too, was a victim of Wes's selfish nature."

Paige set her empty plate on the coffee table and balanced her fork on it. "I, for one, am glad she returned to Texas. Otherwise, she wouldn't have met my dad, and I wouldn't be here."

Cassie and Skye shared a smile. Even Remi's expression held a glimmer of humor.

The stern set to Nash's face lightened slightly.

Remi smiled at the younger woman. "Since Luke's our brother, that means we get you by default." She winked at Cassie. "The women still outnumber the men."

Cassie caught Luke's gaze. His vivid blue eyes shone with hope—a hope she shared. Why was it important for her best friends and Luke to get along? Because he'd put his life on the line for her, and she would always be grateful? Because he was a faithful, hardworking employee? Because he deserved some happiness after the tragedy he'd endured?

"You really should try the pie, Luke. It's your favorite."

Remi looked between him and Nash. "Lemon meringue is Nash's favorite, too."

Nash kicked up a shoulder. "He's got good taste."

Skye smiled. "I'm sure you'll discover you have a lot more than pie in common."

Remi cocked her head. "How did you wind up a detective?"

The nervous energy in the room dissipated, and while Remi and Luke talked about their respective paths to law enforcement, Cassie and the others served themselves dessert and coffee. As soon as Nash polished off his slice, he disappeared into his bedroom and returned with several boxes filled with old photographs. The group spent the next hour rifling through photos. Luke visibly soaked in Nash and Remi's shared memories, some of which were lighthearted and some somber.

Cassie's phone buzzed, and she checked the screen. "It's Detective Kane."

She walked into the foyer before answering it. Luke followed her, his gaze sharp and questioning. She put it on speaker.

"We've taken Carl Jenkins into custody. He had a duffel bag full of large bills in his apartment, the same bag he had upon exiting the hospital. Unfortunately, he's been unwilling to talk."

"You don't have anything to use as leverage?" Luke asked.

"We've offered him a deal. If he hands us the man behind the attack, he'll get a lesser sentence. So far, it's a no go."

Cassie looked at Luke. "Why wouldn't he take it?"

Frowning, Luke shrugged.

"From the little he's let slip, our man spooked him," Kane answered. "Told him in detail what he'd do to him if he squealed."

A muscle in Luke's jaw twitched. "What about the money bag?"

"We're checking it. In the meantime, I'll keep hammering at him."

"What about the Scottish store owner? Did you get anything from her?" Cassie asked.

"She wasn't open to cooperating with me, I'm afraid."

"What do you mean, exactly?"

"She doesn't like cops," he retorted. "I don't have enough to get a warrant and force her to share her security footage."

There was the sound of muffled voices. "Listen, I've got to run down some leads on another case. Be in touch soon."

Cassie stared at the phone, disappointed and frustrated. "Why do I get the feeling Kane's giving the least amount of effort to finding my attacker?"

Luke wore a scowl. "He hasn't inspired my confidence, either."

"His haphazard approach is putting people's lives at risk."

While Kane worked to piece the puzzle together, a ruthless killer remained at large, and no one could predict where he'd strike next.

EIGHTEEN

Luke knocked on Cassie's door before sunrise the next morning, wishing he didn't have to be the bearer of more bad news. Her muffled response was followed by a rustling sound. She opened the door wrapped in a fluffy white robe over her yeti pj's. Her hair was a tousled wave about her shoulders, and he had the urge to smooth it off her creased brow.

He pushed a mug of freshly brewed coffee into her hands. "Sorry to wake you like this, but we have to get on the road."

"What? Why?"

"He's killed another young woman."

Although he'd prepared himself for her response, the terror and guilt stealing over her face was like a gut punch.

"Where?"

"Biloxi. Near the hospital. I saw the online article this morning. Apparently, she's been dead since Monday, and her body was discovered overnight."

Cassie sagged against the doorjamb, and Luke took her mug before she spilled the contents.

"Just like last time. He was prevented from killing me, his true target, and in his fury, he chose another victim."

"It's not your fault, Cassie."

"Do we know anything about her?"

"They haven't revealed that information yet."

"Because they have to notify the family," she said dully, splotches of color high in her cheeks.

"Let's go sit down."

Putting his arm around her, he guided her down the hall and onto the couch. Setting the coffee aside, he sat beside her, took her hands in his and tried to rub warmth into them.

"I can't believe this." The despair in her pretty brown eyes gutted him.

"We're going to nab this guy."

"You don't know that."

There were too many unsolved cold cases for him to dispute her words.

She clung to his hands. "Luke, what if they can't identify him? I can't live in this constant state of fear. I have to go back to work. I have obligations." Her brows dipped in a frown. "You can't stay here indefinitely."

Already, Luke wondered if he'd have a job to go back to. He had plenty of sick time racked up, but the heads of the department were getting antsy and needed him there working cases. He was one hundred percent focused on protecting Cassie, though. He'd told himself it was because she was a good person and boss. He'd told himself he owed her because of his deception. He suspected the reasons went much deeper, but he wasn't going to do a self-examination.

He had to be realistic. Their lives were miles apart geographically. He didn't know how his relationship with her best friends was going to pan out. He couldn't do anything to jeopardize her connection to them. Most importantly, he didn't deserve her, not after how he'd treated her.

"Let's not go down that road, all right?" Releasing her, he gestured to the other bedrooms. "I can't let my sister stay here. I'm going to follow her until she's out of Mississippi. Then I'm going to pay a visit to that Biloxi store

and speak with the owner myself to try and get information on the belt." He stood. "You can go with me, or I can
drop you off at Nash and Remi's. Better not mention what
I'm planning. Kane won't be happy to know I'm following
up on his work."

She stood as well. "I'd like to go with you. I'll make breakfast while you tend the animals."

Luke admired her grit in the face of adversity. She con-
tinually amazed him.

"I'll never forget you, Cassie West."

Her mouth opened and closed.

The tips of his ears burned. He probably should've kept
that to himself.

Luke went to wake his sister. Paige wasn't thrilled to be
disturbed at this early hour. She was even less happy about
the change in plans. However, she listened to reason. When
he left the house, she was already in the shower and Cassie
was in the kitchen.

Breakfast was a solemn affair. They got on the road not
long after. Cassie spent a bulk of the three-and-a-half-hour
drive to the Louisiana border on her phone, answering emails
and trying to complete her FFA tasks remotely.

When they crossed into Louisiana, they took the first
exit promising a variety of gas stations and restaurants.
After a quick lunch together, Luke and Cassie accompanied Paige to her car. He engulfed his sister in a bear hug.
"I love you, sis."

Her eyes were watery. "Love you, too."

"I expect a text every half hour until you're at your dorm."

A half-hearted sigh gusted out of her. "I know. You've
only told me that a hundred times."

Cassie stepped closer. "I'm happy I got to meet you,
Paige. I only wish you could've stayed longer. Please come
to the ranch again when things are settled."

Paige smiled. "I'd love that. Don't forget to visit us, too."

Cassie's smile was wistful. "Maybe someday."

Luke found himself wishing she would come to Texas. He'd love to introduce her to his parents and friends. *Don't get your hopes up, McCoy.*

When they'd said goodbye and were headed to Biloxi, Cassie broke the silence. "I like your sister. Although I wish we could've met under different circumstances, I'm glad she came."

"She likes you, too."

"Her presence at Nash and Remi's was a good thing."

"She knows how to break the ice, that's for sure."

He'd been on pins and needles, not knowing what to expect. His brother and sister had obviously felt the same. It felt odd calling them that, even in his mind. Even knowing the outcome of the DNA test would be positive, he hadn't allowed himself to call them that.

"I think it went reasonably well," she said. "What do you think?"

Luke adjusted the heater settings and air vents. "I'm hopeful we can find common ground."

"With time and patience, I believe you can enjoy a wonderful relationship. Nash invited you to the wedding, didn't he?"

"He did. Paige, too."

Luke appreciated that they'd included Paige and had been kind to her.

"I invited them to visit me in Texas sometime," he added, watching the cars whizzing past on the interstate. "Not to parrot my sister, but I'd like you to come, too."

She slowly nodded. "I'd like that."

Thanks to several traffic snarls, they reached Biloxi shortly before sunset. Lights glistened on the bay, and a giant Ferris wheel glowed neon. The shopping complex was located at the end of a long stretch of white-sand beach between a museum, a sprawling casino hotel and the marina. The only parking to be had was in a five-story garage. The complex had a meandering layout, and shoppers could stroll between the storefronts.

Luke and Cassie accessed the Celtic shop by way of a sidewalk flanked with palm trees. Unfortunately, the restrooms and vending machines were right across from the entrance, and the nearest shop was far enough down that their cameras wouldn't have captured the customers going in and out.

The door chimed an alert when they entered. The counter was smack in the middle of the store, and a brunette woman looked up from her book and smiled brightly.

"Welcome. Are you looking for anything specific today?"

"Actually, we'd like to talk to you about one of your customers," Luke said, flashing his badge. "I'm Detective Luke McCoy, and this is Cassie West. Are you Kathy Sinclair?"

In a blink, her friendliness disappeared. "I am. I've already spoken to Detective Kane. You've made a wasted trip."

"Did he tell you why he's interested in this customer?"

"He only said it was official police business."

The door chimed, and she welcomed the new arrival, although with much less enthusiasm. "Excuse me." She bustled around the counter.

Cassie arched a questioning blond brow at Luke. With his hand on her lower back, he guided her to the side and into the imported teas and cookies section.

"Why the cold reception?" she asked quietly.

"I don't know if it's the badge or the potential for bad publicity. The whole state is up in arms about a serial killer in their midst."

"Or maybe Kane made a bad impression."

She glanced around and nodded to the display in the

corner. He followed her to the leather section, specifically the belts.

"Luke."

He examined the belts in question, his blood running cold.

Her brow creased. "Why did he choose this store and this brand?"

"He could have Scottish heritage."

"Maybe he's traveled to Scotland."

"Or maybe he happened in here one day and liked the products."

Her shoulders drooped. "Random choices won't lead us to him."

Luke looked around and spotted a conspicuous camera. "Kane said Mrs. Sinclair was reluctant to share the footage, and it's doubtful he could get a warrant." He glanced over at the short brunette, who was about to ring up a purchase. "The best we can do is try to convince her ourselves."

After the gentleman left, Luke and Cassie returned to the counter.

Kathy gave them an arched glare. "Unless you plan on buying something, I suggest you be on your way."

"I'm sure you've seen the news about the serial killer on the loose?" Cassie said. "It's entirely possible he purchased several belts from this very store."

Kathy paled and clasped the silver cross hanging from her neck. "The ones he used to murder those women?"

"Yours is the only physical store in southern Mississippi that sells them."

She held up her hands. "I don't want any part of this."

Cassie folded her hands at her waist. "The truth is, Mrs. Sinclair, I'm his current target. I've managed to escape his attacks, but there are no guarantees I'll escape the next one." She pulled out her phone and turned the screen toward Kathy. "See this young woman? She was murdered three nights ago because he failed to kill me."

Kathy stared at the photo in horror.

Luke rested his hand on the counter. "You could be the key to unmasking this monster. Will you help us?"

She released the cross pendant. "What do you want me to do?"

"Can you give us a list of people who purchased multiples of that belt?"

"I can search my point of sales system for dates when the belt was purchased. Unfortunately, I don't keep track of who bought what."

Luke's disappointment was sharp. Many shop owners were now investing in systems that did compile shopper information to help them personalize their experiences and make smarter stocking choices.

"We could look at your video footage on those specific dates." He pointed to her cameras. Most stores kept footage on file for three to six months.

"I suppose that would be all right."

"Thank you," Cassie said emphatically.

Kathy led them into a tight hallway outfitted with a bathroom, closet and office. The office was barely large enough to fit two people, and there was only one chair. Luke hovered in the doorway, and Cassie stood in between file cabinets while Kathy opened her computer program and began the search.

Extracting a spiral pad from the top drawer, she jotted down several dates and tapped the paper. "I sold three during the week before Christmas, all on different days."

"Could be routine holiday purchases," Cassie said.

"True. However, on this day in October, I sold six."

"You don't happen to remember that transaction, do you?"

"I would've remembered that if I'd been the one to ring it up, and I don't. My part-time assistant, Joe Kessler, must've been working that day." The chair creaked as she twisted and flipped through the wall calendar. "There's a red check on the days he worked. See? I was right."

"Will you call him?"

Kathy agreed and contacted Joe. After hanging up, she looked at them. "Joe's not as observant as I am. He only remembers the purchase because the man was wearing a jacket with the hood up, and he thought it was strange due to the warm weather. He doesn't remember any specifics."

Luke wrote down Joe's information and would set up a time to interview him.

Kathy scrounged up a stool for Luke to sit on, pulled up the stored video on the computer and left them alone.

Cassie's breath caught when the man in question entered the shop. She scooted to the edge of the chair, her heart pounding. Although the black-and-white footage was clear, he was wearing a dark, nondescript jacket with the hood completely obscuring his face and hair. He strode to the leather section, chose the belts and took them to the counter.

"He's keeping his head down." Her nails bit into her palms.

"He's obviously been in this shop before and is aware of the cameras. His clothing doesn't have insignias, and I can't see his shoes. Looks like he paid with cash, of course."

"Hold on." She paused the video. "Do you see that? When he hands over the cash, his sleeve rides up and reveals his watch. I don't know much about men's watches. Does it look familiar to you?"

Luke's shoulder brushed hers as he leaned in. "It's not a smart watch. I can't see the manufacturer name, but I'm sure my coworker at SAPD could examine the video."

"How quickly can he review it?"

"I'll relay the urgency of our case. I'll get Kathy's permission first."

Cassie checked her phone and groaned.

"What's the matter?"

"I have several missed calls from Fallon. I completely forgot I was supposed to go to his house this evening and examine Titus's dairy operation." Following Luke into the store area, she motioned to the door. "I have to call him back."

"Don't go far."

Outside, Cassie stood at the picture window and watched a mom and daughter enter the restroom.

"I'm so sorry," she blurted when Fallon answered. "I just now saw your calls."

"Cassie, Titus missed swim practice in order to meet you." Fallon's ire was unmistakable.

"It completely slipped my mind."

"I feel for what you're going through, but your personal troubles are starting to affect my son and the other students. That's not fair to them."

Tears smarted her eyes. She cared deeply about her students, and the last thing she wanted was to let them down. "Please give my apologies to Titus."

There was a beat of silence. "Are the authorities any closer to identifying your attacker?"

"Not yet, but I'm hopeful there will be developments soon. Is Titus free tomorrow evening?"

"I'll have to check with him."

"Thanks, Fallon."

Luke exited the shop and held up a flash drive. "Kathy gave me the footage. I'll get it to my coworker as soon as we return to the ranch." They walked along the sidewalk. At this time of evening, there weren't many shoppers braving the cool, damp weather. "Why were you going to Fallon's?"

"I was supposed to examine Titus's dairy operation and complete a proficiency." At his inquiring look, she continued, "FFA awards scholarships worth substantial amounts of money. They want to know the student is actually doing what he or she claims and deserves the prize. Fallon was angry because Titus missed swim practice to meet with me. He insinuated that my focus isn't where it should be, and he's right. I hope I don't lose my job over this."

Luke stopped short and took her hand, causing her to stop. "You're committed to your students. No one can argue otherwise. You forgot a meeting. So what? You'll reschedule."

"I'm certain there are other staff members who feel the same as Fallon."

He cupped her cheek, and electricity seemed to buzz through her nerve endings. "You are a valuable asset to your school and community. I don't think you realize what a special woman you are, Cassie." His eyes glowed brilliant blue beneath the string lights. "I can tell you right now I wouldn't give you up without a fight."

Cassie's breath whooshed out. Her focus narrowed to the man in front of her, blocking out the upbeat music piping through the speakers, the distant shouts from the Ferris wheel, the swirling scents of salt-filled air, kettle popcorn and hot cider. His lips pressed against hers. Shock blasted through her, riveting her to the sidewalk. Their breath mingled in the cool air. Logic evaporated. Her growing feelings for this man dissolved the mental obstacles. She leaned into his kiss.

It was as light and perfect as a Christmas morning snowfall. His closeness infused her with longing for something far deeper than bodyguard or friend.

Have you forgotten he deceived you, like Brian? Used you for his own agenda?

Her giddiness evaporated. Cassie pushed him away and he immediately let her go.

Questions shouted from his eyes. A pair of teenage girls giggled as they passed, and color climbed into his face.

"I, uh, think I need to eat," she blurted, unwilling to explain her sudden change of heart. "Are you hungry? There's a well-known burger place on the way out of town. We could order food to go."

He stared at her for a long moment before inclining his head. "Sure."

They walked to the truck in silence. Cassie had always disliked parking garages. They'd seemed deserted and creepy to her even before she'd become a killer's target. As they reached the second deck, a brisk wind whistled through the structure, chilling her. A trunk door slammed in the distance, followed by a car alarm. She increased her pace, eager to be inside the safe, warm cab. Luke went around to the driver's side.

She heard a guttural exclamation, followed by a strained shout. "Cassie, run!"

Her thundering heartbeat blocking the sounds in her ears, she raced around to the other side. Blood leaked from the side of Luke's neck as he wrestled with a masked attacker.

NINETEEN

Cassie leapt into the fray, shoving the attacker in the ribs with all her might. His arm sliced through the air, connecting with her chest and forcing her back into the truck. Growling, Luke landed a blow to the side of the man's head, stunning him. Luke reached for his weapon. Before he could release it from the holster, the masked man punched him where blood leaked from his neck.

Luke stumbled into the truck.

The man turned to her, his eyes full of the lust of the kill. She couldn't help Luke by fighting. She had to lure the killer away and give him time to call the police.

Pivoting, she raced toward the ground level. He chased after her. Her relief that he'd left Luke alone was quickly replaced by fear. She ran as fast as she could, yelling for help. But the parked cars were all empty, and no one responded. Emerging from the garage, she saw a family with young children in between her and the shops. Cassie ran toward the marina instead. Ducking into the vacant, open-air pavilion by the water, she glanced over her shoulder. He wasn't there.

Chest heaving, she turned a complete circle, her gaze attempting to penetrate the shadows. Was he there in the nearby marina? Behind one of the columns or the garbage receptacles?

A sudden noise jangled her nerves, and she made for the kid's playground between the pavilion and beach. Ducking beneath a climbing structure, she pulled out her phone and typed a text to Remi.

Danger. Biloxi Waterfront. 911.

A gloved hand reached out, snagged a handful of Cassie's jacket and gave a powerful tug. Screaming, she jerked free, dropping her phone in the process. Coming out the other side, she made for the beach. As her boots sank into the sand and running became a challenge, she wished she'd gone a different direction.

The beach was deserted. No one occupied the picnic tables or benches beneath the trees bordering the roadway.

Cassie was forming a prayer when she was tackled from behind. The hard impact stalled her breath. Sand went into her mouth. He seized a fistful of her hair and hauled her up, propelling her toward the park restrooms. Tears smarting her eyes, she spit out the sand and screamed. Just beyond the restrooms, cars whizzed past on the two-lane road. No one could hear her. No one stopped.

Her attempts to slow his progress failed. The women's bathroom door loomed in her vision.

She was going to die in a bathroom, yards away from help.

Luke would find her cold, lifeless body and blame himself.

Please, God, help me. I can't leave my loved ones or my students behind.

Reaching over her head, she grasped blindly, her fingers snagging his mask. She yanked on it. Muttering expletives, he let go.

Cassie bolted past the concrete building, zigzagging between trees and emerging on the roadway. A horn blazed a warning that jarred her eardrums. Another oncoming car's brakes locked up, squealing against the asphalt. The headlights blinded her, and she held up her hands to brace against impact.

Luke dialed Cassie's number again. There'd been no sign of her at the marina, and no one inside the arcade center had seen her. He kept his hand pressed to his wound, uneasy about the lightheadedness overtaking him. Ringing drew him to the playground. He snatched the phone from beneath the structure. When he straightened, his head spun, his stomach lurched, and sweat dotted his upper lip.

He sank to his knees. *I can't lose consciousness, Lord. Who'll find Cassie? Who'll tell the police what happened?*

He pulled his hand away from his neck and grimaced at the fresh blood gleaming in the lamplight.

Car lights washed over him, and tires screeched. He saw a door swing open, and a figure jump out.

"Luke!"

He sagged with relief, unable to summon the energy to get up and hug Cassie. Instead, he slumped onto his backside, using the slide to prop himself up.

She joined him on the ground and peered at his neck. "Why didn't you wait for me in the garage?"

"Had to find you."

Peeling off her jacket, she tossed it aside and took off the thin sweater she wore over a T-shirt. She folded the sweater, gently dislodged his hand and pressed it against his wound.

"Did you call the police?" Her brow pinched with worry.

"Should be here any minute."

A woman ran up, presumably the driver of the car. "What can I do to help?" she asked, wringing her hands.

Cassie glanced over her shoulder. "The police have already been contacted. They will probably want your account of what you saw. Thanks for the ride."

"Of course. Is he going to be okay?"

"He's going to be fine," she stated firmly. "Aren't you, Luke?"

She skimmed her hand through his hair, tenderly pushing it off his forehead. Concern filled her eyes.

The ambulance arrived, and a pair of paramedics rushed over. Cassie stepped aside to let them assess him.

"Stitch me up here," he said, feeling sleepy. It was getting harder to string thoughts together. "I'm not going to the hospital."

"You've lost a lot of blood."

He looked to Cassie, expecting her to be on his side. She couldn't want to return to the same hospital where she'd recently been attacked.

"It's all right, Luke. I'll stay with you the whole time."

"Sir, we need to get you on this gurney."

"Don't want to…"

Blackness clawed at him, and he was vaguely aware of the paramedics strapping him onto the gurney and loading him into the ambulance. Cassie's voice filtered through his consciousness. The darkness of the waterfront was replaced by eye-burning light. An engine started. Doors clanged shut. They were in motion.

A cold hand smoothed over his forehead and hair.

"Cassie," he mumbled.

"I'm right here, Luke."

He forced his heavy lids open, and her sweet face filled his vision. "Beautiful."

She smiled and caressed his hair again.

An oxygen mask came over his mouth, and the paramedic instructed him to breathe deeply. Awareness of his surroundings seeped in. The IV bag pumping his veins full of fluids. The tape adhering the bandage to his neck. The compartments of medicines, needles, supplies.

He squeezed his eyes closed, certain he could smell the horrendous stench of burned flesh. Memories of the flames, the smoke, the terrible knowledge that his partner was dead rushed in, along with the remembered pain screaming through his shoulder.

"Can't be here," he murmured.

His heart began to strike hard against his chest wall. His breathing became shallow. Was he having a heart attack? He knocked the mask aside.

"What's happening?" Cassie demanded.

"He's hyperventilating."

He felt a flurry of movement around him.

"He was in an accident last year." Cassie threaded her fingers through his and held on tightly. She brought her face close. "Listen to me, Luke. You're going to be fine. You're not in Texas. You're in Mississippi with me."

Luke clung to her voice, her touch, her gaze. She began to pray aloud. By the time they arrived at the emergency room, his panic had receded.

Cassie insisted on staying with him, and the nurse in charge of his care gave her permission. When a police officer arrived, she invited him into the room and gave her statement. Luke, already stitched up and feeling clearheaded, followed up with his own.

"We found a bloody knife at the scene," Officer Daniels told them. "My partner took it in for processing. We also found a tracker on your vehicle."

Luke looked at Cassie in surprise. "We've routinely checked our trucks and haven't found any."

"This one was sophisticated and hidden carefully."

"I wonder how long he's been aware of our movements," Cassie said.

Officer Daniels looked grave. "You should have your other vehicles checked. In the meantime, our guys are speaking with potential witnesses in the waterfront area."

He promised to keep them updated. While they were waiting for official discharge papers, Remi arrived unannounced.

"I've been trying to reach you both," she exclaimed, her face pinched with distress. "What happened?" She strode to his bedside and scanned him from head to toe. "Are you okay?"

Her obvious concern warmed him. "I'm fine."

"I'm sorry I didn't return your calls." Cassie left the chair to stand beside Remi. "I silenced my phone when the police got to the waterfront and forgot to turn it back on. We were ambushed in the parking garage, and he stabbed Luke."

Luke was angry with himself for not anticipating the attack. "I told Cassie to make a run for it. Instead, she tried to defend me and then lured him away."

Cassie propped a hand on her hip. "And you should've stayed in the garage, but you chased after us despite your injury."

Remi glanced between them. "What were you doing there? I thought you were following Paige to the state line and returning home."

Cassie bit her lip.

Luke pulled the flash drive from his jeans pocket.

Remi's brow furrowed. "What's on it?"

"Footage of the serial killer." Her mouth dropped open, and he held up his hand. "We can't see his face. He's too careful for that. But we may be able to get some information about him based on the type of watch he's wearing. I'm going to send it to my coworker in San Antonio."

"Why are you trying to go around Kane?"

"He's not giving Cassie's case priority. He paid a visit to

this same shop and came away with nothing. I'm not about to trust him with this."

"We didn't want to put you in a bad spot," Cassie added.

Remi digested the information. "I happen to agree with you. Kane is distracted by other cases, as well as a situation at home. He's too proud to delegate, however. Or maybe he doesn't yet get that I'm good at my job." She handed back the drive. "Let me know what you find out?"

He nodded, and his neck throbbed with dull pain. The medicine they'd administered hadn't fully kicked in yet.

As he took the flash drive, Remi surprised him by squeezing his hand. "I'm glad you're all right. I'd like for you to stick around a while longer. I mean, I haven't had a chance to tease you yet."

His throat grew tight. He had a lot to live for, a lot to thank God for.

Cassie put her arm around Remi. "She's a pro at it. Ask Nash."

Smiling, Remi gestured to the door. "I guess I'm your ride back to the garage. Does anyone want coffee?"

"I'll take some," Luke said. He wouldn't likely sleep tonight anyway, not after the attack. Not after that kiss.

He much preferred to think about Cassie's sweet lips beneath his, even though he wasn't sure it had been the wisest move. That would likely be their one and only, so he may as well savor the memory.

When Remi left the room, Cassie sat on the bed and folded his hand between hers. Her brown eyes were soft and earnest, and he longed to have the chance to gaze into them every day. Her touch was both comforting and thrilling. The fact she seemed to care about him, despite his selfish deeds, pointed to her pure heart.

"Luke, I think it's time you returned to Texas."

TWENTY

"And leave you alone with a monster on the loose?" Luke demanded, his brows crashing down. "No way."

Cassie had to set aside her own needs. "You could've died. You heard the doctor—a little more to the right, and you would've bled out before my eyes." She couldn't be the reason he didn't return to his family. Tonight, she'd gotten an inkling of what Luke must've felt when Simon died.

"I'm fine." He shifted his legs to the side of the bed and would've gotten up if not attached to an IV. "I got careless, that's all. I'll see the next attack coming."

"Go home, Luke. Before it's too late."

"No."

Cassie stared him down, torn between rejoicing and stomping her foot. Couldn't he see she was trying to protect him? He didn't owe her. He wasn't a citizen of Tulip, wasn't a part of their law enforcement team and wasn't tasked with serving her community.

"I'll kick you off my ranch."

"I'll park my truck at your gate and sleep there."

He was stubborn enough to do it, too. "I'll call the sheriff and complain."

"I'll find another place to stay," he countered grimly. "But that would put you at greater risk. You're not driving me out of town, Cassie West. I'll leave when this guy is dead or in jail."

"And if that takes a year? What if he's never found?"

"I can't think that way, and neither can you."

"One black coffee and peppermint hot chocolate coming up." Remi breezed back in and handed them each a cup. They mumbled their thanks and fell into stilted silence.

She arched a brow. "Did someone turn on the air conditioner? It's chillier than it was a few minutes ago."

The nurse's arrival was a timely distraction. She handed Luke his discharge papers, removed the IV line and bandaged his hand. Thankfully, the hospital was only a couple of miles from the waterfront. The continued police presence alleviated some of Cassie's fear, but she wasted no time getting behind the wheel of Luke's truck and driving them out of town. Remi followed them to the ranch.

"What's Nash doing here?" Luke pointed to his truck parked beside the barn.

Nash met them midway between the house and barn. "Your cattle and horses have been fed and watered. The chickens put themselves to bed."

"You didn't have to do that." Cassie hugged him. "I appreciate it, though. I feel like I could sleep for a week."

Nash tweaked a strand of her hair. "Remi told me what happened. I figured you two wouldn't feel like tending chores."

Gripping his hat in his hand, Luke added his thanks.

Nash squinted at him. "How many stitches did you get?"

"Thirteen."

Nash whistled. "Could've been worse."

"That's what I told him." Cassie gave Luke an arch stare.

"It's over now." Luke hooked a thumb toward the house. "I'm hungry. There's leftover stew in the fridge, right?"

Cassie was sure he was trying to change the subject. "And cornbread."

"I could go for coffee," Nash said.

"You guys go on in the house." Remi linked arms with her. "I left a book at Cassie's."

"Book? Since when?"

She squinted at her. "You don't remember?"

"Oh. Right." Cassie looked at the guys. "Make yourselves at home. We'll be over in a few."

Dusty followed them into her tiny home. Cassie flipped on the lights, filled the electric kettle with water, set it to boil, and then retrieved a box of assorted herbal teas.

Remi got out matching mugs and pulled the sugar bowl over.

"Sure you're not mad about us interfering in Kane's investigation?" Cassie rested a hip against the counter.

Remi flipped her ponytail behind her shoulder and folded her arms across her chest. "I am mad, but not at you and Luke. Kane's work practices have become sloppy in the short time I've been there. He's become distracted, yet he won't let me or the others in our unit assist. I've kept my mouth shut, but no more. I'm going to confront him first thing tomorrow morning."

"Don't jeopardize your job because of me."

"Yours isn't the only case he's fumbling."

"Are you going to tell him about the footage?"

She nodded. "I'll ask Luke for a copy to give to Kane. I won't mention Luke's intention of sharing it with his co-worker. I *will* ask Kane why he didn't get the footage himself."

"Two departments working on it is better than one. I think Luke would agree."

The kettle switched off, and Cassie poured hot water into the mugs.

"What was going on between you two back at the hospital?"

Cassie swished her tea bag and watched color infuse the water. "I told him to go home. He refused."

Remi paused with the spoon in the sugar bowl. "He obviously cares about you. How deep do your feelings go for him?"

"I'm fighting to stay alive here, Rem."

She placed her hand on Cassie's upper arm. "This sort of situation can accelerate a relationship. It happened with Nash and Skye."

"They grew up together."

"They didn't know each other, though."

Cassie refused to examine her heart too deeply. She already knew she'd miss him something fierce when he left. He'd leave a hole in her life. She wouldn't ever forget him, either, not with memories of him stamped on every part of her life.

She discarded the tea bag in the trash and carried her mug to the sofa. Her dog jumped up beside her, circled a few times and flopped down. "Is Patrick still calling you?"

Remi got comfortable on the other side of Dusty. "I'm not finished talking about Luke. You've always been like a sister to me, but wouldn't it be amazing if you married my brother? You'd be an official member of the family."

Cassie's heart leapt at the thought…which was a troublesome reaction. "We can talk about your ex or rejoin the men. Your choice."

Remi scrunched her nose. "Fine. Patrick has finally given up, I think. I hope."

Her friend had returned from Atlanta with a heavy heart and sadness she couldn't seem to shake. Cassie was grateful that Remi seemed to be recovering from her breakup.

She hadn't thought Patrick worthy of Remi, but she'd supported her friend's choice to follow him to Georgia.

Remi blew on her tea and petted Dusty. "I'm sadder about wasting time in a failed relationship than losing him."

"If you learned something useful or grew as a person, then it wasn't a waste of time."

She laughed softly. "You sound like your mom. When are they coming home? I miss them."

"I do, too, but it's safer for them to stay where they are." *Thank You, Lord, for small blessings.* Having her parents here would've made the situation worse.

"Has anyone in the department caught your eye?"

Remi grimaced. "I won't be ready for another relationship for a long time."

Cassie thought back to her and Luke's kiss. Normally, she would've told her best friend about something that momentous. This time was different. She and Luke weren't meant to be.

Cassie walked into school Monday morning full of anticipation and apprehension. Everyone knew the reason she'd been absent last week. How many would share Fallon's annoyance?

The man in question was stationed at his classroom door as usual. His mouth tightened when he saw her, but he waved in greeting.

Luke had accompanied her to Fallon's home Saturday morning so she could observe Titus's dairy operation. While Titus had been his usual affable self, Fallon had been reserved.

Cassie entered her classroom, relieved to be back. The students greeted her with enthusiasm as they entered and found their desks. She took the roll immediately after the bell rang.

"Where's Morgan?"

Jane opened her folder and uncapped her pen. "She's home with a sinus infection."

Cassie was disappointed. She'd wanted to speak to Morgan and gauge how things were going in her life.

The first half of the class was a lecture. Cassie texted Luke their plan when it was time to go to the barns. He'd remained on school property while she worked, even though that meant more ranch work for him in the late afternoon and evening hours.

She pushed the exit door open and almost knocked the maintenance man off his ladder.

"Elias!" She tilted her head back. "Sorry, I didn't see you there."

He kept a steady grip on the upper rung. "No trouble, Miss West."

Moving aside so the students could file past her, she glanced at the cardboard box and the box of tools. "What are you doing?"

"Installing security cameras. I've already put some out at the barns."

"Oh."

Gabriela hadn't informed her that the cameras had been approved.

"Miss West?"

Cassie turned to see Jane waiting nearby.

"What is it, Jane?"

They began strolling along the sidewalk that would take them past the football stadium and to the barn. Luke was in the distance, his eyes shaded by his Stetson and black shades.

"I'm not sure I should say anything." She pressed her lips together. "Morgan told me you found out about her and Vince, so I guess it's okay to talk to you."

Cassie stopped and touched Jane's arm. "You're obviously worried about her. I admit I am, too."

"She's been telling her dad that she's coming to my house, but she's actually going out with Vince."

"I see."

Color flooded her cheeks. "This past weekend, she returned early from their outing. She was crying and wouldn't tell me what happened. That's not like her. She tells me everything."

"Has she seen him since?"

"I don't think so. She wasn't feeling well yesterday."

"Thank you for telling me, Jane."

"What are you going to do?"

"I haven't decided yet."

"I don't want to get her in trouble or have her be mad at me."

"Her safety matters most."

Cassie mulled over her options as they walked in silence to the barn. Luke caught up to her before she entered.

"Everything okay?" he asked.

She relayed Jane's account. "I have no choice but to speak to Evan. I'll wait until after the engagement party tomorrow night. I don't want to ruin their celebration. With Morgan sick, she shouldn't be seeing Vince before then."

"Do you have a minute? We've had a breakthrough on that footage."

She grabbed his wrist. "Really? What is it?"

He showed her a website link on his phone. "See this watch?"

She gasped. "I see the price! Who spends five thousand dollars on a watch?"

"Apparently our killer," Luke said, scrolling to show her more details. "It's a diving watch, water resistant to one thousand feet."

Cassie absorbed that information. "This is huge, Luke."

"It's a small but significant detail. The closest places to dive are Biloxi and Gulfport. We can start looking here." He typed a name into the search engine. "Adventure Scuba. They offer a variety of diving classes and certifications. He may have come through there. Next, we can check out charter companies."

"And if he owns a boat?"

"We talk to the folks docked at the downtown marina."

Cassie shook her head. "It's a long shot, isn't it?"

He settled his hand on her shoulder. "Let's try and stay positive. This could be the break we need."

She prayed he was right. The longer that madman was allowed to roam free, the more people were at risk of getting hurt or killed—and she couldn't add that to her already burdened conscience.

TWENTY-ONE

Luke couldn't keep his eyes off Cassie. Evan and Arianna's engagement party—held in the same barn rental as the high school dance—was in full swing. She'd been swallowed up by a group of women when they'd arrived. He'd found the drink station, helped himself to a glass of iced tea and took up position in the corner, where he could keep an eye on her and the guests.

The red number she'd worn to the dance had knocked his socks off. Tonight, she looked ethereal. Her soft-pink dress had transparent sleeves, a tucked waist and flowy layers to the middle of her calves. The dreamy color, matched by her lipstick and nail polish, enhanced her beautiful brown eyes and made her skin glow. Her hair was secured at her nape in a demure style, and silver earrings skimmed her cheeks. She reminded him of those glamorous, old-Hollywood movie stars in the classic films his mom liked.

Luke would very much like to dance with her again. Hold her in his arms and forget the danger waiting around every corner. Kiss her without doubt, question or misgiving.

"You'd better stop gawking," Nash murmured, appearing at his elbow. "This is Tulip. Rumors run wild with moon-struck expressions like that."

Luke took a long drink of tea before turning to Nash. "Where's your better half?"

"Skye's meeting me here later. Her sister had a rough day, so she spent the afternoon with her."

Cassie had told Luke about the accident Skye and her sister, Dove, had been in when they were teens. Her sister had suffered terrible injuries that had left her in a vegetative state. Thankfully, Skye had gotten her sister into a nearby facility where Dove received top-notch care.

Nash crossed his arms over his chest. "So what are your intentions?"

"Intentions?"

"Cassie is important to us. She's family."

Luke stared down into his glass.

Nash cleared his throat. "I didn't mean to imply that you aren't," he said gruffly. "It's just—"

"No need to explain." Luke met his gaze. "I may not have the history with Cassie that you and Remi do, but I care about her, too."

Nash studied him for a long moment. "I figured you did, seeing as how you've stuck around to watch over her. It's obvious you two have a connection. Brian did her dirty, and you've already hurt her once. Don't leave her with a broken heart."

Luke's gaze sought her out again, and he caught her staring at them with a quizzical expression. Arianna murmured something in Cassie's ear, and the connection was broken.

Nash wouldn't be happy if he heard about that kiss. Neither Luke nor Cassie had dared discuss it in the days since. What was there to say? That he both regretted it and longed to repeat it?

Nash nudged him. "It benefits me if you two remain on good terms."

"Oh? How's that?"

"I expect you to visit Tulip often in the future, starting with my wedding. Lord willing, more children will come along and will need to meet their uncle." He gestured to the entrance, to where Remi was relinquishing her coat to the owner, Mr. Winfield. "It would be good for Remi to have you around, too."

Luke smiled.

Thank You, Lord Jesus, for bringing good out of an uncertain situation. Help us to find common ground and forge strong bonds.

"How's the investigation going?" Nash ran a finger underneath his collar. "Remi told me about her confrontation with Kane."

Remi headed their direction but got sidelined by Sheriff Hines. Luke's admiration continued to climb where his new sister was concerned. As promised, she'd confronted Kane first thing Friday morning. He'd been angry and defensive, but she hadn't backed down. He'd begrudgingly agreed to accept her assistance on the case.

"Cassie and I drove down to Biloxi after school yesterday and spoke with the Adventure Scuba staff. We showed everyone a photo of the watch. No hits. I left the photo to be circulated among the employees scheduled to work later this week."

"Remi was in Biloxi and Gulfport today with Kane," Nash said. "She said the charter companies didn't produce any leads."

"Remi, Cassie and I are going to the Biloxi marina tomorrow after school."

Detective work was slow and tedious at times, especially with a criminal as careful as their serial killer. He was getting less careful as time passed, however. Luke hoped that would work in their favor.

"Can I have your attention, everyone?"

A hush blanketed the crowd as Evan beckoned Arianna

over. When she reached him, she kissed his cheek and leaned into his side, beaming with happiness.

"Thank you for celebrating with us tonight," he continued. "We'd like you all to know how special you are to us. I'm blessed to have found the love of my life." He glanced at Arianna. "We're impatiently waiting for our ceremony in the summer. If it was up to me, we'd elope."

The crowd chuckled.

"However, my bride-to-be likes to uphold traditions, and I will honor her wishes."

Evan wound up his short speech and directed the guests to the supper buffet. As conversation broke out once again, Luke's mind wandered to Cassie and her canceled wedding.

"Nash, did Brian and Cassie have an engagement party?"

His brows tugged together. "Yes. It was an outdoor affair, held on her ranch. Her parents paid for the catering and music. She reimbursed them, even though they told her not to."

Luke hadn't thought about how public her almost-marriage had been. In San Antonio, only those in his circle of friends would know about a breakup. In Tulip, everyone knew. And not just the headline news. They knew details. How awkward it must've been for her.

If he wasn't careful, he'd subject her to similar scrutiny when he left town. He refused to do that to her.

Despite everything going wrong in her life, Cassie enjoyed spending time with her dearest friends. Evan and Arianna were too busy making the rounds to settle on one table, so she and Luke shared a table with Nash, Skye and Remi. They didn't speak of the investigation. Instead, they discussed Nash and Skye's summer wedding and honeymoon plans. The reconnected siblings also used the time to ask deeper questions about each other's childhoods. Cassie was familiar with most of Nash and Remi's stories. She listened avidly to Luke's history, hungry to know more and understand what made him the man he was today.

At the dessert table, they surveyed their options. He handed her a plate. "Is this difficult for you?"

"Is what difficult?"

"Nash and Skye's wedding plans. Arianna and Evan's public displays of affection." He gestured to the tablescape of candles and framed photos of the couple. "The reminders of your past."

"It's gotten easier." She suspected her growing feelings for Luke played a large role in that. "I'm truly happy for my friends."

He chose a miniature serving of banana pudding and a slice of key lime pie. "I've never come close to getting married, but I have to agree with Evan. Eloping sounds easier and less stressful."

Before she could respond, Jim approached. "Cassie, may I have a quick word?"

Luke's expression darkened. "Whatever you want to say to her, you can say right here."

Although Cassie wasn't particularly interested in what the gym teacher had to say, she had to try and keep the peace with her coworkers. "It's all right. We'll be right there by the coatrack."

Luke reluctantly accepted her empty plate.

Over by the coatrack, she crossed her arms over her chest. "What's on your mind, Jim?"

He rubbed his hands together. "It's come to my attention that my behavior has made you uncomfortable. I want to apologize, Cassie. I respect you as a teacher and a friend. At least, I hope we're still that…friends. Are we?"

Again, Cassie strove to smooth things over. "Yes, Jim. We're friends."

"Good." He licked his lips, still rubbing his hands. "Good. You're aware that my wife has trouble coming into town and being around large groups of people. She's lonely. Would you consider maybe paying her a visit sometime?"

The question threw her. At her hesitation, he said, "I wouldn't have to be there. It could be just the two of you. Or bring a friend, like Arianna."

"I'll consider it."

"Thank you, Cassie."

Nodding awkwardly, he returned to his table. Cassie was on her way back to the dessert station when Morgan emerged from the restroom. Her nose was pink, her eyes red and mascara smudged.

"Morgan, honey, I've been wanting to talk to you. Are you all right? You look like you've been crying."

Sniffling, she shot a glance at the closest tables. "I'm okay."

"You don't seem okay." She patted the young woman's shoulder. "Let's go back into the restroom and fix your makeup."

Morgan trudged back inside and immediately burst into tears.

"Sweetie, what's the matter?"

"My life is over."

Praying for wisdom, she put her arm around the girl's thin shoulders until her tears were spent. Handing her several tissues from the dispenser on the counter, she said, "You can talk to me. It might be hard to believe, but I was a teenager once upon a time, too."

She blew her nose. "It's Vince."

"Did he do something to hurt you?"

"No." She blinked fast. "I broke up with him."

Surprise rippled over Cassie. "You did?"

"This weekend. I think you were right. He's so much

older. I don't have anything in common with his friends. He talks about stuff I don't know anything about."

"I see."

"Is this how you felt when your wedding got canceled? Because I don't want to fall in love again. It hurts too much."

Cassie bit her lip. There was no comparison between a teenage romance and her and Brian's lengthy relationship and engagement. Morgan's feelings were real and powerful, however, and she wouldn't discount them.

"The hurt does lessen over time. While it's tempting to try and protect yourself once you've experienced hurt, you shouldn't close yourself off to loving again. Love is worth the risk."

Cassie should take her own advice. Opening one's heart to another person, becoming vulnerable again, took courage.

"Take your hurts to the Lord, Morgan, along with your hopes and dreams for the future. He'll guide you and give you wisdom, if you only ask."

Arianna entered then, and her eyes widened at Morgan. "What's the matter?"

A fresh wave of tears overtook Morgan, and she sought solace in Arianna's arms.

"I should've told you," Morgan mumbled.

"Told me what?"

She pulled out of Arianna's arms and confessed everything.

"You knew about this?" Arianna asked Cassie, her eyes in turmoil.

"Luke and I saw them at the winter dance. I wasn't sure what to do."

"Evan won't be happy. You both let him down."

"I'm so sorry."

"Do we have to tell him?" Morgan said.

"Yes," Arianna said. "You're going to tell him tonight after everyone leaves. Don't worry, I'll be with you."

"Okay."

Morgan left the restroom, leaving Cassie and Arianna alone.

"I truly am sorry, Arianna."

"I know." Arianna's expression shouted her disappointment, which made Cassie feel an inch tall. "You've been under a tremendous amount of stress. I truly don't know how you've handled it all with such strength and grace."

"It's not me. It's God. His strength has seen me through each and every day."

She nodded. "Still, I feel like you should've spoken to us. Morgan could've been in real danger."

Cassie bit her lip hard to keep from crying. Arianna excused herself, and Cassie spent a few more minutes trying to compose herself. When she emerged, Luke was waiting for her.

"Everything okay?"

"Would you be disappointed if we left early?"

"I'll get our coats while you tell the others goodbye."

She pleaded a headache. Outside, he walked her to the passenger side. "Are you going to tell me what went on between you three?"

"Arianna knows that I kept Morgan's secret from them. She's understandably upset, but she gave me a pass because of my *situation*. Ugh, I'm so tired of this!" She threw up her hands. "I'm failing at my job. I'm failing in my friendships. He's ruining my life, Luke."

"We've got a lead—"

"Right. A stupid watch. That's it. This could go on for months. Years. Meanwhile, more women will suffer at this monster's hands."

Her voice broke, and her tenuous hold on her emotions

was severed. Luke put his arms around her, holding her securely as she cried.

"You're going to be okay, Cassie," he murmured. "I'll make sure of it."

She wasn't going to be okay. Even if they did catch the killer, and her life went back to normal, Luke was leaving Mississippi.

Did he feel anything for her beyond friendship? Did the mere thought of being apart make his heart feel as if it had been ripped out of his chest? Did a future without her seem bleak and hopeless?

Cassie stepped back and dashed the wetness from her cheeks. Now wasn't the time to fall apart. She had to stay strong, or at least put on a brave front. She couldn't let anyone know—least of all Luke—that she'd fallen in love with him.

TWENTY-TWO

"Jane, do you know why Morgan isn't here again today?"

After last night's conversation, Cassie had expected her to show for class.

"I messaged her before school and didn't get a response. She wasn't active on her socials last night." Jane glanced at the students sitting around her. "Anyone else heard from her?"

Titus shrugged. "She's been preoccupied with her mysterious boyfriend."

A couple of the students chuckled, and Cassie quickly changed the subject. Between second and third period, she poked her head into Arianna's office. "Morgan's not here. Is she okay? Did she speak to Evan after the party?"

Arianna's countenance still carried disappointment, and Cassie regretted letting her friend down. She had yet to face Evan and ask his forgiveness—a task she wasn't looking forward to.

"She texted that she didn't get much sleep last night and woke with a bad headache. Evan told her to stay home. I was with her when she talked with him. As expected, he was upset." She leaned back in her leather chair. "However, the timing was good, I think. He was in high spirits after the party, and he took it better than I thought. It helped that she's already broken up with this man."

"I truly am sorry I didn't come to you immediately, Arianna."

"I know you care about Morgan as much as I do."

Her words gave Cassie hope that the rift between them could be repaired. The phone on Arianna's desk rang, so Cassie left and returned to her classroom.

After school, she climbed into Luke's truck. His eyes were bright with hope that hadn't been there as they shared lunch.

"Remi texted with news. The man who assisted our killer in the hospital attack has changed his mind. He's willing to talk in exchange for a deal."

Hope exploded inside her. "Really? Oh, Luke, that's wonderful!"

"He likely doesn't know our guy's name, but he can give a sketch artist a description."

"Imagine—we could know what he looks like today."

Luke smiled. "I have to stop by the farmer's co-op before we head home."

"I was planning to ask if you had time for me to swing by and see Morgan."

"We'll go there first."

"It won't take long. I have some assignments to give her."

"You could've emailed those to her. Admit it, you want to see for yourself that she's all right."

She buckled her seat belt. "I'm worried about her. I hope she doesn't change her mind and go back to him."

"I doubt her father will allow that to happen."

Evan's home was located on a country road near the high school. Luke pulled into the drive and parked behind Morgan's old Volkswagen Beetle.

"Looks like she's here alone. It's probably best that you wait out here. She'll be more willing to talk if it's just me."

Luke agreed to wait in the truck, and Cassie hurried to the front door. Morgan answered the doorbell's chime.

"Miss West, is everything okay?" Her brows pulled together at the sight of Luke's truck parked in the drive.

"I brought your assignments from the last three days."

"Come in."

Morgan closed the door and led her to the kitchen. She paused the video she had pulled up on her laptop. Cassie placed the folder on the counter.

"Arianna told me you had that talk with your father last night. How did that go?"

"He's livid," she said flatly. "He took my car keys. I'm grounded for the rest of the school year. He said he *might* let me go to the spring formal, but he hasn't decided yet."

"I'm proud of you, Morgan, and I'm praying for you."

Her eyes watering, she tugged her sweater more tightly around her. "Thanks."

"Have you thought more about what you'll do after graduation?"

"I'm probably going to college like I originally planned."

Cassie smiled. "Just keep praying for God's guidance, and He'll lead you on the best path."

Morgan nodded. Her phone pinged, and she read the text.

"That's Jane. I have to send her a picture of something from my room."

Cassie glanced around the kitchen and attached den. Noticing the framed photos on the built-ins flanking the fireplace, she wandered over. There were several of Morgan as a child, both alone and with her father. There was one of Arianna and Evan on a boat, their arms thrown around each other. The name of the boat was the *Revenge*. Not a typical name.

She started to turn away when she caught sight of a smaller, dustier frame behind the others. With trembling hands, she reached for the photo and picked it up.

The child in the photo was obviously Morgan. The woman was a stranger to Cassie, but the sight of her struck horror in her. About the same height and weight as her, she had blond hair and brown eyes…the same as all the killer's victims.

"I see you've found a photo of Morgan's mother."

Cassie jumped, spun and dropped the frame. The glass cracked.

"Evan. I—I didn't know you were home." Her body was numb, her mind frozen.

His smile was grim, his eyes glittering in anticipation.

It couldn't be Evan. Not Morgan's father. The man Arianna loved and had pledged to marry. The respected veterinarian.

He casually gestured to the door behind him. "I was in the barn, loading supplies into my truck." He strode between the couches and bent to pick up the frame. He stared at it, his mouth pinched. "Georgia was a beautiful woman." His gaze slowly lifted and roamed her face.

Cassie felt as if she were seeing Evan for the first time. The raging hatred in his eyes made her knees go weak. He was the one who'd attacked her in the barn and the school. He'd known her every movement, had followed her to the RV warehouse, injured that employee and coerced a hospital worker to assist him.

What was he going to do with Morgan in the house and Luke in the driveway?

"I was gullible. Taken in by her beauty. I was blind to her scornful, hateful personality." He shook his head. "She looked like a lamb, but she was actually a viper."

"Evan, listen to me—"

He moved quickly, imprisoning her with his arms and pressing a damp cloth over her mouth and nose. Cassie struggled to dislodge him. Soon, her thoughts became disjointed, and she sagged against his chest.

Before she succumbed to the darkness, she heard Morgan enter the room and gasp.

"Morgan," he said over his shoulder, surreptitiously removing the cloth. "Miss West fainted. She's learned that Luke McCoy is the killer the police have been looking for all along. Whatever you do, don't let him in."

Luke checked the dashboard clock again. Twenty-eight minutes.

"Did you hear what I said?" Paige repeated.

He shifted the phone against his ear and studied the house. "Your psych teacher is unreasonable. I heard."

"You don't think it's unreasonable to assign a twenty-page paper due in less than two weeks?"

"You're a bright student," he said absentmindedly. How much longer was Cassie going to be in there? "You can do it."

"The question isn't if I can. It's if I want to. Doesn't he realize I have other classes?"

"It's called time management, sis."

She sighed. "Change of subject. I told Mom and Dad about Cassie and her ranch, and that you invited her to visit us. Mom's face lit up at that. She asked if I thought you two made a good match, as if people actually say that anymore." She snorted. "Anyway, I told her you were perfect for each other."

He tapped his knee. "Paige, I'm kind of in the middle of something. I'll have to call you back later today."

"Fine. I could tell you're distracted anyway. Love you."

"Love you, too."

After ending the call, he texted Cassie.

Everything okay?

A response came almost immediately.

Yep. Sorry it's taking longer than I thought.

A smiling heart emoji popped up, and he frowned.

Cassie didn't use emojis, at least not with him. The heart threw him.

He opened his truck door and stepped out. The sudden arrival of patrol cars, lights flashing and sirens blaring, startled him. The cars blocked him in. Over the loud speaker, he heard a command to put his hands up.

Confused, Luke obeyed. Sheriff Hines emerged from one of the vehicles, and Luke called out to him.

"What's going on, Sheriff?"

"We got a call about an intruder at this residence. What's your business here, McCoy?"

"Cassie's inside with Morgan. I've been out here waiting almost half an hour."

The heart emoji came to mind again, and apprehension shot through him.

"I think she's in trouble."

He dashed to the porch and pounded on the door. The sheriff and Deputy Flowers rushed after him. When no one answered, he peered into the window.

"I see her cell phone! It's on the coffee table."

There was no movement inside. No sound.

His stomach churned.

The sheriff brushed past him and attempted to summon someone. "Police! Open up!"

After what seemed a lifetime, Morgan cracked open the door, her brown eyes large and fearful.

"Morgan, where's Cassie?" Luke demanded.

She stared at him with obvious distrust. Sheriff Hines insisted she allow them to enter, and she reluctantly complied.

Luke picked up Cassie's phone. "Did you answer the text I sent her?"

Morgan folded her arms over her chest. "My father said you're the man who killed all those women."

"Evan was here?" Striding into the kitchen, he saw the barn and outbuildings out back. A gravel track led to a side road, meaning Evan could've left the property without Luke seeing.

"Did you call the police and claim to have an intruder?" the sheriff asked.

"I had to protect Cassie."

Luke reentered the living room, unable to believe what he was hearing. "Where did he take her?"

"I don't know. Far from you." She turned to the sheriff. "Why aren't you arresting him?"

"Morgan, Luke isn't the killer," he said gently. "He's protected Cassie all this time."

"What reason would my father have to lie—" She broke off, her eyes popping out of her head. "You don't think— He would never—"

"Morgan, this is important," Luke said, urgency gripping him. "They left in his truck, correct?"

Her face contorted. "She was sick. He was helping her."

Luke looked at the sheriff. "Call the school and have Arianna come here. She can stay with Morgan while we search."

Luke exited the house through the kitchen door, fear striking his heart. He dialed Remi's number.

"Detective Wilder."

"Remi, I need you." He could barely push the words out of his mouth. "Evan Tucker is the killer, and he's taken Cassie."

TWENTY-THREE

Cassie woke to the jostling and bumping of a livestock trailer. She lay on the dusty turf floor and tried to get her bearings. Her head pulsed with a constant, dull ache. Her stomach roiled. When the truck made a turn, she rolled over and almost lost her lunch.

Disjointed prayers for deliverance and mercy flooded her mind. At the memory of those last moments with Evan, she let out a sob of disbelief. Her heart broke for Morgan. And poor Arianna. Their lives would never be the same. Surely Luke had already discovered she wasn't in the house.

Tears streamed down her face. What if she couldn't escape this time? The thought of Evan winning, of fleeing and never being found, infuriated Cassie. She had never experienced fear on this level before, but she had to fight for herself. She had to fight for justice for all those women and their grieving loved ones.

She had to fight to see Luke again.

She slowly sat up, disheartened to see Evan had put her in the trailer's dressing room. The shiny solid walls offered nothing in the way of escape. Pulling herself up using a saddle holder, she crossed to the door and stared out the small window. She was surprised to see the bustling, downtown area near Biloxi's waterfront.

The boat in the picture—the *Revenge*. They must be headed to the marina.

The door handle didn't respond to her attempts to open it. He must've jammed it from the outside. If only she could get someone's attention...but the window had a dark tint to block sunshine. No one would see her, even if they were stationary.

Desperate, she removed her boot and began striking the glass repeatedly. It was a long shot, but she had to do something.

Minutes later, the truck slowed, and she almost lost her balance as he parked near the water. Sweat popped out on her forehead. Her hands got clammy. Had he heard her? Was he going to end her life and escape on his boat?

The unknowns paralyzed her.

A key jostled in the lock, and the door was thrown open. Evan noticed the boot in her hand. Glowering, he closed himself inside the trailer with her.

She backed against the side and drew air into her lungs to scream.

He lunged and pressed his hand over her mouth. "Don't you dare."

Cassie struggled, repeatedly striking his side with the boot. He brought his military-style boot down on her bare foot, crushing her toes. She whimpered.

"You've been nothing but a thorn in my side," he spat. "I hated you from the day I moved to Tulip. You're just like my ex-wife, Georgia. Acting sweet and self-righteous. A know-it-all who can't keep her nose out of other people's business."

The hatred and rage pouring off the man she used to consider a friend astounded her.

"You were off-limits, of course," he went on. "You were too close to home. And my daughter liked you. But then you started interfering in my relationship with Arianna. I couldn't overlook that."

Cassie shook her head, and he pressed his hand harder against her mouth.

"Don't try to deny it. When you kept the fact that Morgan was dating that dirtbag Vince from me, I knew my decision to bury you was the right one. You were slippery, though. I blame Luke McCoy."

He rustled in his back pocket with his free hand and brought out a cloth. She made a protest in the back of her throat.

"I could kill you here and now, you know. But after all the trouble you've given me, I feel like savoring this moment." He smiled in triumph. "We're going out to sea, Cassie. No one will be able to save you there."

"Can you drive any faster?"

Luke braced himself against the dash of Remi's unmarked patrol car. He had a terrible feeling they weren't going to reach Cassie in time. He regretted not telling her everything that was in his heart.

God, I need her in my life. Please don't take her away from me.

Remi drove with her fingers glued to the wheel. Her face was locked in determination.

"Biloxi PD is closing in," she said, not taking her eyes off the road. "We'll get to her in time."

Despite her shock and disbelief, Morgan had been a source of useful information. She'd shared that Evan owned a boat that he kept in the Biloxi marina. She'd also confirmed that he was a master diver and owned the exact watch they'd seen in the store footage.

Remi and Luke had anticipated Evan's next move and had headed toward the Gulfport and Biloxi area. The fact he had a horse trailer attached to his truck made him easier to track on traffic cams. The Biloxi PD had sighted his vehicle as Luke and Remi reached the outskirts of the city.

Luke received a text from Nash. "Nash and Skye are thirty minutes behind us."

A grunt gusted out of Remi. "I can't believe it's Evan."

"None of us suspected him." Luke was disgusted with himself. The killer had been right under his nose, and he hadn't had a clue. "He had free access to her. He knew her schedule, her habits. Everything."

"But why her? I know she resembles his ex-wife. But why bring attention to himself by singling her out?"

"I don't know."

The faces of Evan's victims paraded before his eyes. Curling his hands into fists, he stared unseeing at the passing buildings, wishing time would slow down and give them a chance to save her.

At long last, they wheeled onto the street by the water, veering into the parking lot where several Biloxi PD patrol cars had gathered around Evan's truck and trailer.

Remi put the car in park, and they both jumped out. Luke raced over, his heart in his throat. Why were the officers just standing around looking somber?

Dear Father, please don't let her be in that trailer... Don't let us be too late.

"Where is she?"

The first officer he encountered attempted to block him. "You can't go over there, sir."

Remi raced up, flashed her badge, and introduced herself and him.

"Truck and trailer are empty," the officer said.

Luke's knees almost failed him. "Where'd they go?"

He turned a complete circle, hoping for a sighting of her blond hair.

"Truck's still warm," the officer replied. "They couldn't have gone far. We're searching for witnesses."

Luke wasn't going to wait around. "I'm going to the marina."

"I'm coming with you." Remi indicated her bulletproof vest. "First, you put on one of these."

Luke took the one she pulled from her trunk and quickly put it on. Jogging to the waterfront path, they hurried past a vacant brick building with their weapons drawn. The marina was within sight, the boats bobbing in the water.

A man and his dog headed toward them.

"You're police, right? I saw a man chase a woman into that building." He pointed to a boat mechanic shop.

"How long ago?"

"Couldn't be more than five minutes."

Luke scoped out the two-story cement building. The sign indicated they were open for business. The rear entrance faced the water, with parking in the front. No way to gauge how many people might be inside.

Together, they approached the single metal door and found it unlocked. He entered first. Several aisles of shelves greeted them. To their right, a boat being serviced was in the middle of an open space. An oversize garage door, currently closed, provided access to the outside.

A crashing sound ricocheted through the building. Using hand signals, Remi let him know she would proceed along the far aisle. Weapon raised, he entered the open space, his heart hammering in his chest. He bent to look beneath the boat and shelving units on the opposite side. Continuing between the boat and shelves, he noted a bathroom, the door thrown open, and an office.

As he approached the office, he locked eyes with an elderly man crouched beneath a desk and halted. The man wasn't wearing a uniform. His eyes were terror-filled.

Luke put a finger to his own mouth. The man nodded and pointed over his shoulder, indicating the direction Evan and Cassie had gone.

Remi caught up to him and followed closely behind as he forged ahead. He paused at the stairs with a sign indicating the cashier was upstairs. He glanced back at Remi, brows raised. Her forehead creasing, she shook her head. Luke nodded and continued past the aisles. Up ahead, daylight filtered in, and he glimpsed a bank of windows and another metal door.

His gut hardened. Had they already left the building?

A woman's cry reached his ears. Before he surged ahead, Remi tapped his shoulder and pointed right. He nodded and advanced to the open area ahead, careful not to make a sound. A grunt, followed by a loud crash of what sounded like tin cans hitting the cement floor, spurred Luke to rush ahead.

He rounded the last aisle just as Evan seized Cassie from behind, holding a metal bar to her throat.

"Drop it!" Luke ordered.

Cassie's frightened gaze snapped to Luke, emotions flooding the brown depths.

Evan's fury was redirected at Luke, and his face contorted. He looked nothing like the affable, small-town veterinarian he'd presented himself to be. The man who'd proclaimed his love for his fiancée had been a façade. This was the true Evan Tucker, a man who thrived on killing, on deciding women's fates.

"The only way she lives is if you let me leave with her."

He started backing toward the door, using the pressure of the bar to force Cassie to move with him. She held it tightly, as if she could prevent him from cutting off her air supply.

"Can't do it, Tucker." Luke took one step, then another. "You deserve to pay for the pain and grief you've caused."

To Luke's right, several filing cabinets blocked the view of the end of the nearest shelving unit. He was counting on Remi to come through for Cassie.

Evan got closer to the door and escape. "You don't have a choice. I know you care for her."

Cassie's eyes got big.

"You're right, I do. I also care about justice being served." He sidestepped several toppled paint cans.

"You have a choice to make then," Evan said. "It's Cassie or me. You can't have both."

Remi emerged from behind the filing cabinets and pressed her gun to Evan's head. "Seems we can," she drawled. "Release her. Now."

Evan stilled, his gaze darting around, seeking an out.

"Morgan knows what you are," Luke stated. "Arianna knows. Soon, the entire nation will know your face and your name. There's no escape this time, Tucker."

Locked in a standoff, the seconds ticked past like years. Sweat trickled beneath Luke's collar, and his muscles screamed for release. What would Evan do? How desperate was he?

Slowly, he lowered the bar from Cassie's throat, ultimately dropping it to the floor. With a cry, Cassie ran to Luke. He caught her to him with his free arm, holding his gun steady on his target.

Remi holstered her weapon, handcuffed Evan and pushed him to a sitting position on the floor. After notifying the nearby police, she looked at Luke. Something unspoken passed between them, and he nodded in understanding. In that moment, he knew he could trust her. She knew the same about him. He and his siblings were going to be okay.

But what about him and Cassie?

Holstering his gun, he framed her dusty, grimy, beautiful face with his hands. "Are you all right?"

Her lips trembled. "Thanks to you and Remi, I am."

Law enforcement officers burst onto the scene and took custody of Evan. As soon as they vacated the building, Remi rushed over and threw her arms around them both. The women shared tears, and Luke's eyes were suspiciously wet, too.

"Thank You, Jesus, for Your kindness and mercy," Cassie whispered.

"Amen," Remi added, lifting her face to smile at Luke. "We make a great team. Sure could use someone like you in my department."

Luke returned the smile. Adrenaline fading, his mind was slowly grasping the truth… The enemy was no longer a threat. The danger that had hung over them for weeks was no more.

"May I have a moment alone with Cassie?" he asked his sister.

Her smile widened, and she patted him on the back. "Take all the time you need, big brother."

When Remi had gone, Luke cradled Cassie's cheek with his hand. "This isn't the time or place to have a momentous conversation, but I can't wait any longer. These past weeks have confirmed what the garage fire and Simon's death taught me. We aren't guaranteed tomorrow. I can't let another minute go by without telling you that I love you, Cassidy West."

She gripped his waist on either side. The residual fear leached out of her face, replaced with joy and wonder. "You do?"

Lightly caressing her cheek, he smiled down at her. "I don't want to live without you, Cassie. I want a future with you. Do you think you could learn to trust me again?"

A tear slipped from her eyes, and her smile was tender and loving. "I already do. I know the man you are, Luke

McCoy, a man of courage and deep feelings and loyalty. I also know you aren't perfect, and neither am I." Going on her tiptoes, she brushed his lips with hers, making him catch his breath. "I love you. If you walked out of my life, you'd take my heart with you."

Joy dissolved the last of his doubts, and Luke kissed her, pouring his love into the embrace and leaving no question in either of their minds that this was meant to last.

He lifted his head. "So you'd be okay if I relocated to Tulip?"

She laughed. "I'd definitely be okay with that."

They got lost in each other's arms again, oblivious to the world around them, thankful for the beauty God had brought out of ashes.

EPILOGUE

The last day of school never failed to fill Cassie with a mix of emotions. While she looked forward to the slower pace of summer, she would miss seeing her students every day. For the seniors, this marked the end of an era and the beginning of new adventures. This year was particularly poignant. Morgan, Titus and Jane would graduate in a few days. Her time with them had come to an end, and her heart ached a little because of it.

As she made her way from the barn to the classroom for the very last class of the year, she smiled as she took in the blue, cloudless sky and tender green grass stretching as far as the eye could see. Being able to roam freely about her school campus without worrying about lurking danger was still a novelty. Although Evan would be in prison for the rest of his life, the havoc he'd wrought on their small community wouldn't soon be forgotten.

In the weeks after the news broke, media crews from across the nation had camped out in their streets, vying for interviews with her, Arianna and Morgan. They'd eventually left when none of them agreed to talk and the news cycle moved on to other sensational headlines.

Morgan had suffered the most. The poor girl had shared a close relationship with her father, and she was having difficulty reconciling his heinous crimes with the man who'd raised her. Thankfully, she and Arianna had found solace in each other's company. Arianna had been tempted to move away, but she'd chosen to stay and let Morgan move in with her for the rest of the school year and beyond.

As horrific as this past winter had been, God had brought good from it, blessing Cassie with a love that had taken root in the worst of circumstances. After Evan's arrest, Luke had given notice to his department and applied for a spot with the Mayfield police. Within a few weeks, he'd gotten the job and moved into a rental house in Mayfield. He and Remi were excited to be working together.

Luke had taken Cassie to meet his parents during her spring break. They were lovely people, and they'd promised to come and visit over the summer. His mom was eager to meet Nash and Remi, as well as Cassie's parents, who'd returned from Florida after Valentine's Day. Her parents adored Luke almost as much as Cassie did.

Entering the building, she nodded at Fallon standing in his doorway and went inside her room. The class was full—surprising given it was the last day. Seniors usually didn't show. The excitement in the room was electric, and she smiled as she crossed to her desk. The surface was piled with chocolates and gift cards from the students.

Jane raised her hand. "Miss West, the seniors made a video for you. Can we play it?"

Touched, she removed the remote from her desk and turned on the television. Jane did something on her phone, and the screen came alive with photographs and footage from the past four years. Her throat got thick as good memories paraded before her eyes. There were humorous moments, as well as ones of friendship and personal successes. When the screen went black, she turned to the students and prayed she wouldn't cry.

"This is a special gift. I'll treasure it always."

Morgan displayed a smile that had been rare in recent months. "There's more."

Brow creasing, Cassie faced the television again. This time, the footage was more recent. The students were lined up at the school barn and holding white posters. One by one, they lifted their posters. Each one had a single letter. W-I-L-L Y-O-U M-A-R-R-Y M-E?

Cassie's pulse bucked and kicked. There was movement behind her, and everyone held their collective breath as Luke strode between the desks with a bouquet of red and pink roses. Cassie pressed her hand over her mouth. He looked dashing in a black suit, his hair slicked back and his face freshly shaven. His eyes were locked on her, his mouth curved in a nervous smile.

When he reached her, he kissed her cheek—drawing giggles from the girls—handed her the bouquet and got down on one knee. His gorgeous blue eyes shone with love for her.

He took her hand and brushed his thumb over her knuckles. "Cassidy West, you're the love of my life. Will you spend the rest of your days with me?"

Tears streaming down her cheeks, she cradled his cheek and dropped a kiss on his lips.

"Is that a yes?" one of the boys called out.

"Yes!" Laughing, she held out her hand and watched as Luke slid a diamond ring on her finger.

"That means we'll have to call you Mrs. McCoy." A junior boy shook his head. "That'll take some getting used to."

Luke grinned, stood and hugged her. "I can't wait to make you my wife," he whispered in her ear.

She grinned up at him. "I'm impatient, too."

"I don't want to steal Nash's thunder," he said quietly. "We should elope. We could have a party for friends and family in late summer."

Although she had no doubts Luke would show, she

wouldn't mind skipping the traditional ceremony. "I'm game if you are."

Joy and surprise stole over his handsome face. "Saturday at the courthouse?"

"I'll be there."

There was a commotion at the door, and Luke turned to his brother and sister, who'd entered the room. "She said yes! Time to celebrate."

After being smothered with hugs from Nash and Remi, Luke led her and the students to the cafeteria, where it seemed the entire school and staff had gathered. Cassie's parents were there, along with Skye and Eden. Hundreds of cupcakes surrounded a giant sheet cake that said Congratulations, Cassie and Luke.

The well wishes carried more weight than usual, probably because everyone knew how close she'd come to tragedy. They also knew about her canceled wedding and were rooting for her and Luke's happiness.

Remi caught her alone, right before she took her first bite of cake.

"I'm so happy for you." Her eyes danced, and she clasped Cassie's upper arms. "I'm happy for me, too. I can't believe you're going to be my sister-in-law!"

Sooner than you think, Cassie thought, giddy at the knowledge she would be Luke's wife by week's end. "You know, with Nash and Luke about to be married men, it's your turn to settle down."

Remi tossed her head, her high ponytail bobbing. "There's plenty of time for that. We have two weddings to pull off."

Cassie stuffed a bite of cake into her mouth and nodded, her gaze sliding to her fiancé near the kitchen. He was chatting with Nash's and Cassie's parents. Catching her gaze, he winked and grinned.

Remi's brows came together. "My brother looks like the cat who ate the canary. What gives?"

Cassie adopted an innocent expression. "It's too soon for you to know his expressions that well."

"I'm good at what I do." Folding her arms, she leveled her gaze at her. "You didn't answer my question."

Cassie hadn't ever been good at hiding things from Remi. Thankfully, Luke swooped in and saved the day.

"Excuse us, sis. I need a moment alone with my bride-to-be." Luke guided Cassie out into the sun-drenched courtyard and beneath the shade of a nearby tree.

"That was close," Cassie said, leaning against the trunk. "I'll have to avoid Remi this week."

"A good reason to spend all your free time with me." Smiling that smile he reserved just for her, Luke rested one hand on her waist and leaned in. "Have I told you lately how utterly gorgeous you are?"

She laughed and glanced down at her collared shirt and jeans, dusty from working in the barn. "I'm just a regular ole cowgirl."

"There's nothing regular about you," he murmured, his voice rich with affection.

Closing the distance between them, he convinced her with his kiss. His lips were intoxicating, and she was glad the tree was holding her up. When he lifted his head, she wrapped her arms around his neck and tangled her fingers in his hair.

"Who would've thought I'd grow up to fall in love with my best friend's long lost older brother?"

"God works in mysterious ways."

"He sure does." She tugged on his collar. "Kiss me again, cowboy."

* * * * *

Dear Reader,

Luke and Cassie's story is the second in my new cowboy suspense series. I'm having fun in Tulip, Mississippi, and I hope you are, too. I'm planning future stories tied to this town and the Wilder family, so be sure to check my website at www.karenkirst.com for updates.

Secrets can be devastating, and their fallout can affect more people than we imagine. When I started this series, I had the idea to include a long-lost sibling. The scenario promised many twists and turns and a strong emotional element.

It's interesting that both Luke and Cassie were hurt by others' secrets, yet they both later chose to keep the truth from people they cared about. In Luke's case, he concealed his true identity from Cassie. And then Cassie kept the news of Morgan and her older boyfriend from Arianna and Evan. It gave me a chance to highlight the importance of forgiveness, because we all make mistakes and have regrets. I'm grateful that God forgives us when we fail Him, and He's faithful to us even when we aren't faithful to Him. Thank You, Jesus.

To find out more information about this and other series, please visit my website. I'm also active on Facebook. You can email me at karenkirst@live.com.

God Bless,
Karen Kirst

COMING NEXT MONTH FROM
Love Inspired Suspense

ALASKAN WILDERNESS RESCUE
K-9 Search and Rescue • by Sarah Varland
A search for a missing hiker goes disastrously wrong when K-9 search and rescuer Elsie Montgomery and pilot Wyatt Chandler find themselves stranded on a remote Alaskan island. Only they're not alone. But is this a rescue mission...or a deadly trap?

DANGEROUS TEXAS HIDEOUT
Cowboy Protectors • by Virginia Vaughan
When her daughter is the only witness able to identify a group of bank robbers, Penny Jackson knows their lives are in danger. Escaping to a small Texas town was supposed to be safe, but now they must rely on police chief Caleb Harmon to protect them from a killer bent on silencing them...

DEADLY MOUNTAIN ESCAPE
by Mary Alford
Attempting to find a kidnapped woman and expose a human trafficking ring nearly costs Deputy Charlotte Walker her life. But rancher Jonas Knowles saves her, and they work together to locate the others who have been abducted. Can they survive the onslaught of armed criminals *and* the perilous wilderness?

TARGETED FOR ELIMINATION
by Jill Elizabeth Nelson
A morning jog becomes an exercise in terror when Detective Jen Blackwell is ambushed—until her ex-boyfriend Tyler Cade rescues her. Only someone is targeting them both, forcing Jen to team up with the park ranger to uncover the mystery behind the attacks...before it costs them their lives.

WYOMING ABDUCTION THREAT
by Elisabeth Rees
There's only one thing stopping Sheriff Brent Fox from adopting his foster children: his adoption caseworker. But Carly Engelman has very good reasons for caution—all of which disappear when the children's ruthless biological father returns to abduct his kids...with revenge and murder on his mind.

SILENCING THE WITNESS
by Laura Conaway
Avery Sanford thought she was safe in witness protection...until her photo was leaked in the local paper. Now vengeful cartel members are on her tail and only former army commander Seth Brown can help her. But with assailants anticipating their every move, can Avery trust Seth to keep her alive long enough to testify?

———————